Darkness

CW00864826

Contents:

Darkness

Darkness

Maybe.
Maybe the choices we make are interdependent. Or
maybe they disappear into a sea of crystal ice
and despair. I've learnt not to regret anything,
however difficult it prevails to be.
I was only young. Young enough that my ignorance
could be excused and glossed over.

Darkness

My name is Elektra.

I am 19 years old.

I hadn't even been born when the world fell into
darkness.

They talk very little of the day the lights went
out; it is almost as if the world underwent a
mind wipe, removing any memory of that day.
Well, it seems more interesting that way I
think. You know stupid conspiracies about little
green men in spaceships with futuristic

Darkness

technology powerful enough to destroy the
planet. Even these days people believe that
Taurus faeces.

My parents talked about their theories a lot.
They believed it was some kind of retribution
from some cloud deity. They were kind of
religious fanatics or something; I don't know,
whatever it used to be called. That was before
they went. Went or died; is there any difference
between them now? The answer to that is a
resounding no. They're dead. They're dead and I
have accepted that; I was only young when they
disappeared into the great abyss that is the
world. They left me so why the hell should I
give a damn whether they still travel this
mortal coil?

I'm not being harsh. I don't think I am. They
left a nine year old child to fend for herself
in this world, without any form of protection
and not even a pot in which to piss.
The world in which I live is different from the
old world, from what I can gather. After the
power lines died on the day of darkness,
humanity fell into chaos. I mean people began to
insane, murdering people for generators and for
any form of energy that would restore their
gadgets and gizmo's. People began to try and
restore the power lines to no avail.
However, people decide to move into the cities

Darkness

from the countrysides, which lead to the
overpopulation of the cities. When the virus
came, poor buggers didn't stand a chance against
it. Everyone was so close. So close. If it had
been a bacterial infection, they still would
have been screwed due to the rise of antibiotic
resistant bacteria. At least that's what I
think. Me and the rest of the living population,
I guess.

Looking out of the window, it's a pretty sorry
sight to be honest. Most of the buildings have
fallen into disrepair. Their foundations cracked
into minuscule particles and debris everywhere.
It's difficult to imagine a world where there
were not buildings falling to pieces on every
street. It's almost possible to see dust spores
floating away from the scene, as if snowflakes
from the sky. I sometimes wonder what it must be
like for those who were born before the death of
society. They have a comparison. Something to
yearn for and memories of a better time. A well
on which to draw.
Oh god, I sound so pedantic.

This flat's not too bad I guess. I could have
got a lot worse from the camp but I guess being
a star pupil had and continues to have its
advantages.
The flat stinks. It stinks of putrefied fish and
stale cigarettes. When Erin, my key worker,

Darkness

first introduced me to this monstrosity I
gagged. Nowadays, I'm lucky to have this place
so I don't tend to complain too much because I'm
always reminded how lucky I am and that I should
be grateful to not be on the streets. That is a
good point. The décor is typically garish, with
damp stained yellow chequered wallpaper in every
room. It looks like someone has 'phlegmed' on
the wall. It's vile but it's almost comforting
in some respect. I feel like that woman in that
novella about insanity and yellow wallpaper. I
can't remember what it's called...oh yes, The
Yellow Wallpaper. I commend the author on her
imaginative title. I'm kidding, kind of.
Well...anyway that is not important.

All of the furniture had been subject to fire
damage and general ageing. The wood has begun to
rot and there is a painting about a vase that no
long exists. Just a gold frame stands where a
canvas image should occupy. In the bedroom, the
bed is tattered and the duvet ripped. To be
honest, the duvet is covered in all kinds of
stuff. I mean urine, crap, blood (I do not want
to imagine where the hell that came from) and a
substance that I am pretty sure is vomit. I hope
it's vomit. Vomit is a best case scenario,
that's not a statement you hear often. There
have been a few times where I have sat down and
thought how many people died in that bed? How
many people died, gasping for breath and calling

Darkness

out for someone or something?
To think about that is not right. To think about
that is not decent and could drive me into
physical insanity. I'm done with that kind of
useless crap; I am alive, that's all that
matters to me. Should matter.

The doorbell doesn't ring often. So whenever it
does, it breaks my chain of thought. What I
actually mean is that the doorbell is so ancient
that it will only work on occasion. I haven't
replaced the battery in weeks and that thing was
decrepit anywhere. So when it does ring, I get
slightly worried because it means that someone
has hammered the crap out of it to work or, I
prefer this option, the stupid, bloody thing has
decided that it likes me today. I walk over to
the door, which I must say is barely attached to
its battered hinges. I never like the feeling of
opening doors; it must stem from some traumatic
memory of school or something but, I still hate
it. Solitude is my only salvation. I relish in
it. That is not strange, I am not strange.

As I open the door I can't hide my disdain.
Roman.
"Hey Ellie, I have not been able to stop
thinking about your beautiful face and your
endless scruples..."
"What do you want, you dickhead?"

Darkness

I don't mean to be snappy but my tolerance only serves me to an extent. Roman and I have never seen eye to eye. This may be partially down to the fact that he is 6ft 4 and I am a regular height at 5ft 5. However, I don't want to agree with him on anything. He is a misogynistic, narcissistic bastard with about as much personality as a cadaver. So I am rather indifferent towards him. Sarcasm fully intended.

"Ah, did someone wake up on the wrong side of the mattress? Aw don't scowl at me like that princess. You know you love me really." He flashes me his most charming grin, as he always does when he wants something badly enough.

"First thing, I slept in the armchair so it is not possible for me to wake up on the wrong side. Second thing, call me 'princess' again, I will not be responsible for your injuries. What do you want Marius? No offence but I want to spend as little time in your presence as is possible." I say with a tone of unmistakable spite.

"Really, all that hostility. My poor heart. I was just wondering...if you happened to have a first aid kit. One of the girls fell. Lot of blood. I have it all under control of course but I would appreciate the kit." The smile does nothing but irk me.

Darkness

You probably think that he's a decent guy, that
I am being too harsh on him because after all,
he gets off his arse and looks after the youth,
right? He only does that to suck up to his boss;
he's hoping by doing a good deed he'll be
recruited for the research team which he has
been rebuffed from many times already. He
genuinely believes he will be the one to
discover a cure for the virus and he will save
the Earth. This is exactly why he deserves the
title of narcissistic git of the decade.

"You know, first aid kits are extremely valuable
these days. You want my kit, I'm coming with
you. It is not leaving my sight. Comprende?"
"Of course, even better. Come along my dear;
patrol starts in five."
"I'm not your 'dear', dickhead." I mutter.
He's so unctuous he makes my skin crawl.

Darkness

Chapter 2

If the view from the inside was bad, walking
through is abysmal.
The constant smell of rotting corpses, dust and
disinfectant.
If the smell wasn't overpowering enough, the
blood covered walls and floors certainly are.
It's like living in a blood soaked world which
makes my dingy little flat seem like blessed
sanctuary.
"When was the last time you left the flat?"
"About a month ago; I went for a massive haul

for supplies before the storm picked up and I had no occasion to leave. I was quite enjoying being alone until you reared your ugly head."
"Aw, don't be like that. You know you only insult me because you want me."
"Shut up. Dumb-ass"
"Bitch."

We always go through this routine whenever we are stuck together. He tries to flirt with me and I shoot him down like an infected. Many of the people at the camp believed that Roman and I would end up together. You know, settle down and raise a family during the end of days.

How bloody pedantic.

We walk quickly.

England did always have a reputation for being the rainiest country in Europe; it still lives up to its reputation after all this time.
I never liked the rain. Even as child. While other children when out playing and splashing around in puddles, I was perfectly happy to just sit and watch under shelter. This may have been one of the reasons why the other kids were always so cautious about me; I wasn't exactly the definition of a normal child. I was pensive and lonely, not vibrant and playful.

Darkness

I am completely freezing; another reason I hate
the rain. The rain feels piercing against my
skin. Even my jacket can't keep me warm any more
which means I need to chuck it away. Crap.

"I starting to think you were on to something
Ellie. Staying inside. Out of the rain and sleet
and snow." I hate a man that can make himself
laugh.
"Yeah, I'm a genius. You should have established
this by now."
"I wouldn't go quite that far dear. You're
nearly there but not quite at my level yet.
Don't worry, I'll get you to that level one
day." He giggles. Complete and utter dick head.
"Oh yes, of course. You are a genius but we all
know what you think with, don't we?" Oh yes, I
win.
"Touché. Touché."

We finally reach the old civic office. It became
a base about a year back and, it serves its
purpose. It contains tonnes of files about the
old days and proposals for what to do when stuff
went bad. They actually believed that they could
survive everything. Arrogant bastards, thinking
they were above everything. We found a few of
their festering corpses when it was discovered.
They must have been dead for a number of years;
it scared the crap out of the kids.

Darkness

I can hear the kid screaming from here. How stupid can you get? Talking is dangerous enough these days and all this kid is doing is drawing attention which puts everyone at risk. It does frustrate me but then again, I don't like children anyway. I never have and never will.

As soon as we walk into the meeting room, the culprit becomes apparent. Little Annie Stoker. Maybe I should give the girl a break, she's only just turned 12. She's so small for age; at her age, I was a lot taller and I had more of an athletic build. She is tiny and is just a sack of bones which is a dangerous thing in this world. In addition her injury does look moderately bad, I guess. Almost half of the skin on her leg is missing and her other leg lies at an odd angle.
When I broke my leg, I didn't cry or scream out. I was 10 years old. I had snuck out to go on a supply run, I was trying to rebel and prove that I wasn't just a defenceless child. I was a stupid bitch then; I should have relished in my youth but then again, in this world being stupid and a child gets you or others killed.
Anyway, I was scoping out this old supermarket that sat at the end of this dead end road. It was quiet, as always, and there was a back window that led directly to the stock room which had been pillaged over the years. However, there was still some medical supplies and food rations

Darkness

so it was worth the risk. There was a rusty
ladder always propped up against the window; I
had done this before and I had been fine, the
ladder had always been secure. That day, not so
much. I was just about to climb in through the
window and the ladder fell, shattering like
glass when it fell. I couldn't pull myself
through the window. I thought I was going to
die. I was about 20 ft above the ground. I tried
and tried to muster the strength to no avail.

I had to let go. I was stupid and reckless so I
deserved to die. The fall was fast so I didn't
have time to think, just to fall. The feeling of
falling was almost liberating, it was like
flying but with a more permanent destination. I
didn't want to land but gravity is a bitch. I
heard the crack of bone and felt the searing
pain of both a broken limb and a shard of the
rusty ladder piercing my back. For a moment, I
thought I had been paralysed. I thought that I
was going to die at the age of 10 after trying
to prove I was a grown up but I lived. I slowly
repositioned myself onto my stomach and tried to
muster a slow crawl. It was agonising and every
move I made, I felt the shard digging its way
into my back and my leg cracking but I had to
continue, I couldn't stop.
The only thought in my mind was: "Oh crap, John
is going to be so pissed. Maybe I should just
let myself bleed out because the lecture I am

Darkness

going to get is going to tremendous." I know
ever the voice of optimism, even as a child. The
shard, due to the fact it was so rusty, should
have given me tetanus in addition to the lovely
tear across my spine. I guess I got lucky in
that respect. When I finally made it to an old
bench that lie in front of the store front, I
finally examined my leg. There was little I
could do about my back with out killing myself
or having eyes in the back of my head. My leg
was a bloody mess. My bone was sticking out and
blood was soaking my jeans. I had to sit and
think about my next move. I noticed a stick at
the foot of the bench; it was the only way I
could attempt to walk back to the camp. What I
did was reckless, impulsive and doltish so I
needed to be lectured. To be perfectly, I was in
too much pain to focus on the minute details.

When I made it back to the camp I went straight
to Rita, the camp nurse, and she tended to my
wounds, using antiseptic to try and stop me from
dying of an infection.

I had never seen John so angry. I was lucky I to
ever leave the compound again.

Annie just continues to sit there, wailing. I
almost feel sorry for her but I cannot allow
sentimentality to overwhelm me. I didn't have to
be there; I'm only here for the safety of my

medical kit.
"Hey Annie, you're going to be alright now.
Ellie and I are here with bandages, antiseptic
and paracetamol. Let's do this." Roman always
has had a way with kids; he's always known how
to calm children down. He bends down to inspect
the wound. It is obvious from here that there is
no compound fracture, just a broken bone which
makes matters easier. He gently touches her leg.
"We need to bind the leg and then attach a
splint so we can get her back to camp. Ellie,
could you bandage her up?"
"Yeah, I guess. Do you have a splint?"
"Don't worry, I'm on it buttercup. Lucy, could
you go and get a stick from outside, preferably
quite tall? Thank you honey."

Lucy Tailor. Reckless and totally infatuated
with Roman, which is slightly paedophilic
considering she is 13 and he is 22. I think she
would follow him to the ends of the Earth; he
says he doesn't notice but I think he just
enjoys the attention.

I sit down and take the bandages out of my
rucksack. They aren't in the best condition but
they will do; I always get nervous at this point
in case I do something wrong. I can do this and
I can do this with as little pain as possible
for both people involved.
"You ready Elektra?"

Darkness

I guess I'm going to have to be.

Darkness

Chapter 3

After filling Annie up with enough Valerian to
knock out a horse, it was peaceful. Too quiet.
All of the other kids are just sitting; they're
in shock which is natural. I'm not in shock
because I'm detached, which I've always
admitted. When I see people dying on the street,
I just walk on by. When people have begged me
for help, I have turned away in the interest of
self preservation. I'm a cold hearted bitch and
maybe that's why I hate Roman so much.

We carry Annie back to base camp; there's barely
anything of her and it feels as if she is
getting lighter by the second. The only

Darkness

comparison I can give is like carrying a rag
doll. A rag doll with a broken leg. Roman keeps
looking over at me; I think he wants me to do
something. React in some way whether it is
crying or puking or destroying something. The
normal reactions when something bad happens. I
couldn't even cry when my parents didn't come
home. When I was ripped away from my home. When
I killed my first infected.

"You okay? You did good back there. I never knew
Rita taught you how to apply a tourniquet? You
are just full of surprises, ain't ya."
"There are a lot of things you don't know. I
used to help Rita in the medical bay whenever I
had spare time, she wanted me to replace her if
something happened. I used to spurt off bull
about her living forever. Let's face it if
something happens, she'll be the first to die."
"What the hell? Seriously Ellie, how can you say
that? Rita has always been there for you and you
can say something so callous? You really are a
bitch!"
"Shut up. You want an argument, wait until we
get back. We are not fighting in front of the
kids. There are more important things at the
moment like Annie, she's still not safe. So
just...shut...up."
"Fine. This isn't over. I cannot believe you
sometimes you know that, you bloody ice maiden."

Darkness

It isn't harsh or callous. Rita is a doctor so
it stands to reason that if there is an
outbreak, she will die. She's not strong or a
fighter. She's smart, incredibly intelligent but
that is not enough. I'm not ashamed to say, if
she became infected, I would put a bullet in her
brain without thinking about it. It's the
kindest thing.

Once we get to the camp, I'm taken aback.
Nothing's changed. There is still a roaring fire
visible by the open window. Lines of fresh linen
possessing the garden like the first fall of
snow. It looks so out of place, with its
surroundings. It reminds me why I could ever
call it home. It doesn't even look like a camp.
The building used to be a care home before
everything went to hell. Oh, the irony kills me
too.

"Well, if I had a pound for everytime I came out
here to see you two, I'd be a millionaire. But
then again, I ain't got no use for that anymore,
eh?"
A small, Asian woman waits in the doorway. Rita,
chief medic and all round mother figure. She
looks tired.
"Rita, how are you darling? Elektra and I were
just talking about you, weren't we dear?"
"Oh really, all good I hope. Why were you
talking about me? You know it makes me

suspicious."
"Nothing, it's not important, is it Roman? We
were just discussing how we need you to check
over Annie. Hence why we're carrying her. And
we're covered in blood. That's was the hint."
Rita is the only one who gets my sarcasm; heck,
she taught me everything I know about being a
sarcastic mare.
"Well, I am getting blind in my old age. A
tourniquet, I'm impressed. You did learn
something from me then."

Looking at her sickens me. It's been four months
since I last saw her and she seems to look
worse.
The black bags underneath her eyes have become
darker. She probably hasn't slept in weeks. Her
skin sagging, her crow's feet more pronounced.
She walks with a cane. It's obvious that she has
been smoking like a chimney recently, which
means something bad has happened. Probably to
one of the kids. She swore to me she would stop;
even the end of days is not an excuse to bugger
up your lungs. There's enough things out there
to make you suffer with out having your body
fight against you. I hate what she does to
herself.

Roman and I carry Annie through to the living
room where an operating table lay, complete with
a saline drip and a trolley full with medical

apparatus. It's not a lot but it's kept everyone alive at the camp, for the moment at least. Watching Rita with a patient is like watching a duck in water. She's in her element with a scalpel in her hand.

"Still going on the basis you would kill her?"

"I have to be prepared to. We all do. It's the only thing we would have the power to do. Roman, if the infection enters this camp, everyone will die. I've seen it before and so have you. You can't be ignorant to that fact; you will have to kill her if something happens."

"I know, I know. I am prepared, kind of. But the way you say it, it's like you don't even care. I envy the way you can just detach yourself from everything. Not feel pain or anything. Why the hell do I envy you? A cold Jezebel?"

I'm sure I can see tears, streaming down his face in the light of the fire. It's so strange for me to see a fully grown man, crying. Men are supposed to be strong but Roman...he's so different to them. He may be a fighter but he feels. He cares.

"First time I've been called a Jezebel. God, are you crying? Are you sure you're not the one with a vagina?" I pause. " You shouldn't envy me. I hate being the way I am; you think not feeling anything is a blessing? It's not. It's like I'm not human anymore; I would love to feel more but

Darkness

I can't because it hurts even more when you lose
them because everyone dies eventually. That's
why I can say that I can kill her."

I walk away.
This is one of the only times I have ever
confided in Roman. Huh, I guess that tragedy
does bring people together. It's a cliché but
like all the best ones, it's true.
When I enter the first room at the top of the
stairs, emotion overwhelms me. My old bedroom,
exactly as I left it. Books on the desks, torch
with its batteries scattered across the floor.
My 12" inch blade. John kept it the same; he
didn't let another one of the kids take my room.
It's almost as if he was waiting for me to come
back eventually. It's just the little things
that get to me; John does care about me in some
regard.
Silence pervades the air like a pariah.
It's at this moment, I feel so alone. The thing
is I do care. I do what has to be done but it
does hurt. The prospect of the only parental
figures I have really ever known terrifies me; I
can't lose John or Rita, it would destroy me
completely. See, I'm not entirely sick in the
head.
I can feel my eyes welling up.
I feel emotionally exhausted and I just want to
forget.
Forget Roman. Forget Rita and John. Forget the

Darkness

world.
But I can't. The only way I can is to shot up or
end it all. I could just take the blade and
slice my jugular. How can I do that? Have one of
the girls come in to find me, bathing in a pool
of my own blood. The poor buggers are scarred
enough already with out finding an old room-mate
topping herself.

The first tear rolls down my cheek. I never
allow myself to feel so weak, at the mercy of
emotion but I can't control myself. I can't stop
the tears flowing and it's not long until I
start hyperventilating. I cannot cope.
There's only so far being the tough little
soldier gets you and it's not far enough.

Darkness

Chapter 4

The morning brings with it a sense of solemness.
I must have cried myself to sleep; just like I
did when I was a child. On a positive note, I
now feel numb which is better than feeling the
ache of loss and clarity. I don't know if I can
face going downstairs, seeing the kids. Seeing
Rita and John. Seeing Roman.

I finally gain the strength to get up. I look in
the cracked mirror that hangs crookedly in the
corner of the room.
I look like crap. My eyes are puffy and my face
is smeared with blood; I must have rubbed my
face during the night. I look like hell. My hair
is sticking up in many different directions. My

Darkness

eyes. Even though my eyes make me look like a pig, my eyes are still piercing. Everyone used to comment on my eyes; my eyes are bright green with flecks of grey around the pupil. My best attribute according to Roman; they suit my ice queen persona.

I enter the bathroom and fill up the sink; it can't be later than 6 am, meaning I have time before the kids wake up. My appearance is like a deranged savage. The cold water cleanses my skin; I haven't realised how warm I am and the freshness of the water feels like being reborn. I can be pedantic too.
After scraping the last of the blood off of my face with a rough flannel, I head downstairs. My god, I am hungry and I ache; the bed did always used to kill my back. I try to make my footsteps as soft as possible, trying not to wake anyone but it was useless. John was waiting at the bottom of the stairs.
I move slowly, his eyes following me, studying me. I am anxious to approach him but then again, I shouldn't be. His grey eyes seem to stare into my soul. Finally his gravelly undertones begin to make their appearance.
"Now, what the hell do you think you're doing, madam?"

I run down the stairs at him; my chest aches with longing. I have missed him so much. He is

Darkness

the closest thing I have ever had to a proper
father, well at least, the only father I have
really ever known. He takes me in his arms and
embraces me. I have missed his musk and his
strong grip. He was the reason it was a little
harder to leave the camp, he didn't want me to
leave but he wanted me to be safe and protected.
I think he understood that the safest thing for
me is to be by myself. But I have still missed
him the most out of anyone.

"You know the usual, getting into as much
trouble as possible. Would you expect anything
else from me, you old git?"
"Walk with me, Lecci. I'll get you caught up on
everything you've missed. You've lost weight and
have you got taller or have I shrunk? Come along
goose."
"No, you've shrunk. What have I missed?"

We walk through and sit on the chairs that lay
in the kitchen. Cobwebs still cling to the
ceiling and there are still numerous cracks in
the marble counter tops.
"Coffee?"
"I could kill for it, thanks."
John gets up and turns the tap on. It takes a
while before the water flows through the pipes.
The pipes always make a weird gurgling sound
when water flows. I always used to think that
was the sound of a monster that was coming to

Darkness

get me, to kill me. Those were the days when I
was still so naïve. Monsters do exist but not in
the conventional form. They exist in all of us.
Sometimes they lie dormant for years and other
times, they appear from birth. We're all
monsters.

"Roman bring you here? Sometimes I think that
boy just looks for an excuse to be with you. I
know he does, you shouldn't tease him."
He breaks into a real belly laugh, from the gut.
He knows that it embarrasses us both, he was the
one who thought we'd be shagging by the time I
was 17. How bloody wrong he was.
"Yeah, Annie got hurt. He needed help applying
the tourniquet. And I know he does; I am just
that desirable ,right?"
"Well, the boy seems to think so. I've always
thought he wants to bang you like a drum..."
"Could we please change the subject? I do
believe I am blushing. You know what a massive
prude I am...that's why you're doing this, you
bastard. Anyway, how's Annie? She was out last I
saw of her, Rita was working her magic."
"It's difficult, she's still asleep. The break
was pretty bad, not as bad as yours was but
pretty close. We've been running low on food
recently so we are all pretty weak, it's
difficult to know if she is strong enough.
She'll probably be fine but there is still that
chance."

29

Darkness

"Oh I see. At least you're honest. Why didn't
you tell me? I could have gone on a run for you,
make sure there were enough supplies. Why didn't
you tell me?"
"There was no point, goose. Runs are becoming
more dangerous and I thought we had enough to
keep us going if I missed meals and I
mean...Rita had her cigarettes so she wasn't
eating. I'm sorry, it's my fault if something
happens to her...if she's not strong
enough...like Isla..."

Silence reigns. I don't know what to say to
John; he's a proud man who doesn't ask for help.
I have always looked up to him; admired his
strength but this reminds me how vulnerable he
is. He's not as young as he used to be; he's
turning 60 soon. He's no longer the youthful man
of action who didn't need guidance or pity.

The whistling of the kettle is the only thing
that breaks the silence.
"What happened to Isla, John?"
"She got sick. Came into contact with the
infected somehow. Rita had to put her down, put
her out of her misery. Maybe if she'd have been
stronger, she might have fought it off..."
"No, don't you dare say that! Nobody fights the
virus off John. No one ever survives, they just
become weaker and sicker and more pathetic.
There was nothing that could have been done and

Darkness

there is no point in blaming yourself for
something that is that far out of your control."

It's pathetic reassurance but it's all I can
muster. Isla was his niece. His own daughter had
died early in the days of darkness. She was one
of the first John knew who perished due to the
virus, the first being his wife. Isla was a year
younger than me. She was only a baby when her
parents were murdered for a small quantity of
tinned fruit and powdered milk. John raised her
as his own, trying to protect her from the
inevitable. He has lost more than any of us. Now
that Isla's gone, I don't know how he will cope
and that frightens me.

I don't know what to say. Most people would say
'I'm sorry for your loss' or some other cliché,
as if it's their fault. My relationship with
John has never permitted that; he doesn't want
sympathy or any bull.
"One sugar, you still like it like that, don't
you? I forget these things. God I miss having
milk in coffee; I've been thinking maybe trying
to find a cow or something. We've got enough
room in the back garden. What do you think?"
"Yeah, yeah good idea. John, you don't have to
pretend you're okay. I know you better than
that; Isla meant the world to you, she meant a
lot to all of us. Why didn't Roman tell me about
it?"

Darkness

"I am okay, as I've always said, everyone dies
and we have to be prepared for that. I don't
think he wants to accept it. They were close in
her last few weeks and I think they genuinely
connected in some way. He pretends he's okay but
everything is starting to get to him. He wasn't
born for this world but then again no one is."

Roman and Isla had always been close. Isla was a
conventional beauty with wavy blonde hair and
pale blue eyes while Roman was the tall, dark
and handsome stereotype. I'm not denying the
fact he is attractive; he has dark brown
shoulder length hair and honey coloured eyes. It
was almost like they were perfect for each other
and they seemed to compliment each other,
personality wise. She was naïve and stubborn
while he was open minded and courageous, a real
hero to her. When he wasn't chasing me like a
little lost puppy, he would spend most of his
time talking to her and to be honest, I think
getting his leg over on her but that was never
confirmed. Isla's death should devastate him to
the core but why wouldn't he say anything to me;
she was like, I use the term loosely, a friend
to me.

John and I sit, just drinking our coffee in
silence. It's true what he says, that everyone
dies and we have to be prepared. I mean I live
by it but I know he doesn't believe it really,

which makes it even more painful.
A pair of footsteps and a tuneless whistle break
the silence. Trust Roman to be the one to break
a dramatic pause. On the upside, he's perked up
since last night, probably trying to forget
everything that has happened. However, his eyes
are still puffy like mine. There's no way to
hide his little masculine breakdown last night.
"Ah John, Ellie and how are we this fine
morning?"
"...Alright. Since when are you this chirpy at 7
am, boy? I usually have to use the ice bucket
method to drag you from your bed. Is it because
of our little visitor?"
"I'm getting taller than you, old man. I'm sure
it's nothing to do with me, right Roman?"
"Of course it is, I'm always chirpy when
surrounded by my ladies. Ah, you brewed coffee,
this is why you are my favourite person Johnny."
"Call me Johnny again, I'll beat your arse you
idjit. Get a cup and sit yourself down...and put
your tongue back in your mouth, you'll attract
flies."

I do love the way John doesn't take any crap
from Roman; I'm starting to see where I get it
from. Ha, I got it from life, I don't need to
blame my glorified mentor.
It is amazing how he can pretend like nothing
has ever happened; I envy that. I catch Roman
staring at me with an unfamiliar expression. Oh

god, I think it's pity. Oh that is sickening,
the only thing stopping me punching him is the
fact that Isla is dead; she was always a
pacifist. That's the reason she's dead. She
resigned herself to just letting things happen
which is suicide, signing over any power you
have over your own life.
I cannot stand people pitying me, like I'm
pathetic or weak. I'm not and I hate people
treating me like I am. Maybe I should be less
defensive about things but I cannot stand the
silent shout of 'you deserve my pity and
sympathy'. I hate it, I hate it, I hate it.

John senses something. I know he does; he is a
good judge of people and interaction. It's not
possible to be warring and for John not to have
the intuition to figure it out. He winks at me,
as if to say he knows what is going on.

"Alright, 'fess up. What's going on? I may not
be the brains of Britain but you kids aren't
discreet. Come on, I do love a bit of gossip."
"Nothing Johnny, I'm just gazing upon the face
of an angel. Nothing more, doesn't she look
radiant today?"
"Flattery never gets you anywhere, boy. Now
what's really going on and cut the crap."
"It doesn't matter; we just had a conflict of
opinions, last night. Nothing important, right
Ellie?"

Darkness

"Yeah, nothing important. Water under the bridge."
"Alright, I'll get it out of you at some point. Now, you going to stay here and scrounge food or are you going to earn your keep?"

I can't help smiling.
"Right you are sir, what do you need me to do; I don't need an excuse to get away from the flat."
"Ah goose, you could move back here; I mean, we have the room and your room is intact and I'm sure the lads could use a role model to teach them how to get things done..."
"No, my flat is mine. Might as well make good use out of it; I'm sure Roman is teaching them sufficiently. When he's not trying to get off with the teens."
"What are you talking about Ellie? I feel like an army general and...hey I do not try to get off with teenagers, they just admire me..."
"Yeah, right. The girls' ovaries practically explode when you enter the room. You say you haven't noticed but I think you get off on the attention."
"Oh piss off, just because you're jealous."
"In your dreams, douchebag."
"If you two are done flirting, it's time to go to work."

Time to go to work; oh it's going to be a long day...

Chapter 5

There's this old saying that John used to repeat
when we were younger: 'calamity is the
touchstone of a brave mind'. I never used to
understand what it meant; it was cryptic as John
always was. Now I understand. It is at times of
crisis that the great and courageous are
separated from the sheep in wolf's clothing. I
have learnt this so many times and yet human
nature still perplexes me; people will always
put up a front to mask themselves from the
world, they will pretend to be stronger than
they are to fit in. It sounds hypocritical
coming out of my mouth.
John would always spout off old proverbs when we
went on a run. I think it was his way of
reconnecting with the time before everything
went to Hell. The stories he'd used to tell
about the days when Christmas lights lit up

Darkness

Trafalgar Square, illuminating a city that never seemed to sleep. When commuters would wake at the crack of dawn and cram onto packed trains and the tube. When the world seemed to be alive. It would be mad not to yearn for that type of a world; instead of the perpetual silence that has fallen.

Roman and I walk in silence out of the front door; John has sent us on a run to get more supplies, I can be persuasive when I desire to be, and I still cannot contemplate everything I have seen and heard over the past day. To think I thought solitude was the best thing for me; maybe I am needed.
I am dreading what Roman is going to say next, he can't stand awkward silences. He is a lot more eloquent when he expresses himself than I am.

"So medical supplies...food...yeah, cool. Wait, they had tonnes of supplies; I saw the medical cupboard. I do believe we have been had by the old codger; I guess we'll just have to talk instead."
"Really, I'd prefer to get supplies. Not that I find your company dull but I find your company dull, with the greatest of respect."
"If you will insist on being a bitch about it. I really wonder what goes on inside your skull, you know that. Nothing phases you, does it? Not

killing people, not the prospect of death, not the idea of people you love dying. It can't be easy but I guess John has got you well trained in that ideology, am I wrong?"
"I guess you're not. I think I've proved things do phase me, I'm not a sociopath. I just want something to take my mind off of things. Like Annie and Isla..."
"Who told you about Isla? She's not dead, she can't be. Rita said she was but she couldn't be because she was Isla and I was supposed to protect her and..."

Roman inhales and places his head against the crumbled wall that stood before us. He begins to hit his head continually until he begins to bleed and he begins to resemble Frankenstein's creature.
"Roman, stop. Stop. It wasn't your fault, it's nobody's fault people become infected. We all know the risks and you shouldn't have to bear the weight of her death. Que sera sera. For god sake, stop it! Do you need me to rohypnol your arse."
"I still had responsibility for her. It was still my fault; you wouldn't understand. She was pr..."
Roman takes one look at me and falls like a log. You bash your brains in against a wall hard enough and you're going to faint, naturally. But he was going to tell me something which seemed

important. He was disorientated so maybe he was just a little delusional but just him to knock himself out when things are getting interesting.

I have to continue on without him. He should be fine if I leave him here; I can't wait for him to wake up and he will be fine. I just have to get a few things and if he wakes up while I'm gone it won't be difficult to find me; I really don't want to sit and watch his dumb ass.

I walk down the road. I shouldn't feel guilty, he'd do the same if it were me lying on the concrete. I can't think about it, I can't.

The sky seems somewhat darkened by the clouds, threatening more bouts of rain; absolutely fantastic. It still looks like it could be dawn but it has to be somewhere about midday. I can see why the world misses clocks, they make things so much easier when deciphering time. I still have my wrist watch but it's been battered to hell. It hasn't told the time in years but I've still kept it, I guess for the sake of being sentimental. It used to belong to my dad from what I can remember. Or it might have been my mum's. It gets more difficult to remember my past. As far as I'm concerned, my life began again when John took me in. There was no real life before otherwise I would yearn for it, wouldn't I?

Darkness

After 5 minutes, I reach my favourite goods
supply; the old supermarket responsible for my
broken leg and a literal stab in the back. You'd
think I wouldn't have ever come back after that
'trauma' but I got over it. The promise of
feeding people is worth getting over your own
crap. It looks even worse than ever; if I'm not
mistaken, it looks like there's been a fire here
recently due to the fire damage and white smoke
bellowing from the building. Crap. I'm guessing
that's all the supplies up in smoke which means
I am up the creek without a paddle. I just have
to hope that there are some supplies that are
salvageable. I mean the fire may have not
affected the stockroom; oh God, I am so screwed.
Why are people such dickheads? Everyone's got to
survive, for god's sake we need each other or
we're all going to end up as worm meat.

I have some rope in my backpack which I always
keep in there in case I need to climb, which is
the most common, or stem bleeding. Who knew rope
had so many uses? Oh, that would be everyone
that has survived thus far.
I throw the rope through the small opening in
the window. My throwing is pretty bloody
amazing, even if I say myself. I make sure the
rope is secure by tugging it; I have learnt my
lesson in regards to unstable climbing
apparatus. I really can't afford to be disabled

at the current time but I have a choice.

Climbing up the wall never gets easier; I pride myself on my abdominal strength so how the hell do the others do it. Oh wait, they don't because they lack judgement.

Once I reach the destination, I realise how difficult this is going to be. There is still a small fire blazing in the centre. The gap in the window seems slightly too small. The last time I went to this supply haunt, I was a few pounds lighter and smaller in general. It must have been a year since I graced the building with my presence. Shit.

I struggle. The gap begins to look like the space is sufficient but it will be a tight squeeze. Damn having muscle; if I was just a skinny little wretch I would not be hanging with my head and upper torso in the building and the rest of me hanging in mid-air attached to the rope. Oh god, I am going to have cuts on my hips by the time I'm through.
Crap, crap, crap. My belt is stuck. My sodding belt is stuck.
If I wasn't so busy using my hands to steady me, I would be able to detach it somehow. Maybe it's a blessing that Roman knocked himself out. I don't think I could live with the shame of Roman always talking about the time he saw me with my

trousers around my ankles while performing a belly flop into a building. Uh, the shame. The shame.
If I move one hand, I can keep a hold of the rope with the other. I just need a few seconds. My only issue is if I drop my belt, there goes my knife. If I get into any shit, I am dead. Well, at least without the belt, I have a chance.

Yes. The belt is detached. Okay, one last push.

Ow. All I can say is...ow. I was right. My hips have been cut to pieces. I look back. There is a significant amount of blood. I'm going to have a fun time tonight; picking out splinters with blunt tweezers. Damn, I need a disinfectant otherwise I could get an infection which could lead to septicaemia which is not something I need to worry about right now.

I let out a little wince. Great...no weapon and now a trail of blood; it's like Christmas.
The fire doesn't appear to be near any of the supplies, which worries me. The last time someone set fire to a building with supplies it was a statement. It was saying: 'if I can't have these supplies, you can all starve with me, you bastards.'
History does have a tendency to repeat itself which is why this worries me.

Darkness

What are they trying to burn?
Purification by fire? Torture?
Oh god Elektra, what the hell have you got
yourself into?

"Get down on the ground! Drop any weapons and
get on the ground!"
Damn. Shit's about to hit the fan.

Chapter 6

"I don't have any weapons. Easy, easy. I'm getting down; it's okay, don't do anything irrational."
"Shut up and just get down bitch!"
I kneel down on the ground slowly, trying to formulate an escape plan. I have no physical weapons but if I can get him on the ground, I can make a clean break for it. Nobody has to get their bones broken. I shouldn't of left Roman. I'm not new to confrontation but it's always ended in blood.
That's when I spot it. A shard of metal shelving. If I can reach it then I have some form of leverage, a way to make this confrontation fair and not one sided.

Darkness

"Give me everything you have on you and I won't
have to slit your pretty little throat. Nothing
personal but I have people to feed so hand it
over. I will kill you, make no mistake."
He is right behind me. Close enough for me to
smell the odour of stale cigarettes masked
slightly by mint. I have always hated the stench
of cigarettes and my coffee is threatening to
make a reappearance; if I am about to die, I'm
going to spend my last moments with a little
thing I call self-respect, not in a pile of my
vomit.

"I understand. People to protect but really...do
you have to kill me? I don't have anything on
me; I don't travel with my supplies so what
would be the point in killing? The group I'm
with will be royally pissed if you harm me.
We're a big group, fifteen strong and I'm sure
you don't want to start anything, do you?"
I edge closer to the shard. He hasn't noticed.
At least I think it's a he; if it isn't a man,
god give that woman a lozenge. I'm not
technically lying about the size of my group; we
are a group of fifteen, but ten of them happen
to be under the age of fourteen. Plus, they
would be pissed if one of their most proficient
hunter, gatherers were to vanish or to be put
out of commission.

"Oh really? I don't give a shit about your

group. I need supplies and if you ain't gonna
give me what I want, I guess I'll just have to
kill you..."
He pauses in the middle of his sentence as if he
is trying to subdue a cough. He turns his head
momentarily and begins to have a violent
coughing fit. Every cough seems to intensify, as
if with every cough he suffocates more. When the
coughing begins to calm, I hear him bring
something up. The reflection from the shard hits
me like a tonne of bricks. Blood. He's brought
up blood.
Oh my god. He's infected.
I am trapped in a blazing stock room with an
infected with a gun to my back...typical
Saturday afternoon.

If he's coughing up blood, he's pretty far along
which means in a day or so he will die choking
on his own blood, struggling for breath. I
cannot stay here. The longer I stay here, the
greater the chance of becoming infected myself.
He's reloading his gun. I have a few seconds.
This is good; I can do stuff with a few seconds.
I just have to strike.
I dart at the shard. He notices this and shots
at my abdomen. One of the bullets finds a way
into my stomach. Getting shot hurts a lot more
than I remember. However, there is an exit wound
which means that I'm going to bleed more
profusely but it is likely to be cleaner, at

least that's what Rita said. The bastard's really going to get it now. I was going to let him go but now...how can I?

I crawl over to the shard. I block everything else out, especially the searing pain in my gut. I grab it. It is relatively sharp but whether it is effective as a weapon still is to be seen. All I can see is a red mist. So I dive at him, knocking him off of his feet. It is dangerous to be in such close proximity to an infected but I don't really give a crap at the current time. It's either him or me and he's close to death anyway. I'm not planning on becoming worm meat just yet.

From what I can tell, he didn't come prepared. He only had three bullets in his gun; all of them are gone. Two in the ground and one that ripped through me. He grabs hold of my arm and tries to twist it. I lift up my other arm, which I had been using to put pressure upon my wound which would stem the bleed, and punch him in the face. I hear a crack; I think I just broke his nose as a great deal of blood flows out of it. He lets go of my arm.

I should leave. He's relinquished his minuscule claim on me but I can't. I can't take the risk that he might leap at me again or might try to find me. No, I have to make sure he can't be a threat. He's heading for the grave anyway. I'm trying to think of it as a form of involuntary euthanasia.

I stand.
He grabs my foot.
I act on impulse.
I lean down and I...I ...I slit his throat.

The look of shock haunts me. I must have hit an artery because I am greeted with an initial jet of blood. I've stabbed and shot people but never have I used blood loss as a weapon. I've always been kind before; I've always delivered bullets and stab wounds to the head or heart, leading to a fast, almost painless death. The blood leaves his body as water spills out of a bucket. He makes a few sickening gurgling noises and then falls unconscious. He won't feel anything. He's already suffocating.

I just sit, in shock.
I just killed someone in cold blood. No, I killed him in self defence. He was going to kill me but I acted first.
Just as promised, my coffee makes its glorious reappearance.
It definitely tasted better on the way down. Now it just burns like bitch.

The adrenaline has began to filter out of my

system and now, my bullet wound really begins to become agonising. I need to get supplies and get back to Rita. An exit wound at close proximity means that the bullet has ripped through me. I am already sitting in a pool of my own blood. I drag myself up. I walk over to the shelves and grab a couple of tins. There's very little left; no medical supplies or anything really useful. Tinned food is starting to become the only consumable food item. Most medication has expired which makes it more dangerous to get ill these days. Unless you can manufacture drugs, you need to grow some form of medicinal herbs if you want to stay alive.

I can't help looking at the assailant. He's wearing a balaclava and he has a rucksack a few metres away from his corpse. Maybe he has something useful on him. I need the supplies more than he does. I walk over to the rucksack; he has a few bottles of water and a pack of handgun bullets. I open the box. So that's what ripped through me. It's not too large meaning the damage is likely to be minimal. No food. I take the rucksack anyway, I need something to carry my loot. I walk over to the corpse and pick up the gun.
I'm tempted to take a look at his face. The face of the man I murdered. No, I can't. I don't want to see him. I prefer to have his identity blank. An anonymous victim.

Darkness

I walk over to the window. The place can burn
for all I care. I secure the rope around my
waist. It kills but maybe it can stem the bleed.
I don't know if I have the strength to try
without the rope. I feel like I am going to pass
out. The amount of blood I've lost, it's only
natural I'm becoming a little hazy.

I finally reach the ground. The tug of the rope
brings a little consciousness, enough to become
aware of things. Pain is a fantastic thing for
clarity.

I have to get back to Roman. To the camp.
I pick up my backpack from beside the bench and
I walk on. I don't have the strength to try and
get the rope back. It's going to burn anyway so
it's not like I am giving somebody else an
advantage.

I begin to stagger home. My head is so faint; I
can't concentrate. Everything aches and the pain
is consuming me. I am near the street where I
left Roman. The bags are beginning to fall off
of my back but if I trying and pick them up, I
may not get up again. I need to stay awake. I
can't collapse because if I do, I'm dead. For
good.

The fact that there is an exit wound means that

there is nothing to stem the bleed; I can only
hope that little damage has been done but I
doubt that. It must have hit something, organ or
bone. It hasn't gone through my spine otherwise
it would have been instant paralysis.

I can't. I'm going to faint. I'm going to faint.
I have to find a place to sit so I don't fall
and hit my head. I don't need brain damage on
top of everything else.
Oh god. Oh god.
I can't hold on.
If I can just get a little further, I may be
alright. Along this road, there is nothing but
concrete. Maybe Roman is still there. I can do
this. If he is still there, I may be okay. Huh,
the only time I have actually wished for Roman
to be there to scoop me up in his arms. Flash me
a charming smile. Tell me I'm going to be fine.
Oh god, did I actually just think that?
That's how you can tell my brain is being
deprived of oxygen. I think I just threw up in
my own mouth. If I'm going to die, I might as
well keep my sense of humour, the only thing I
can control.

I can't. I can't hold on. Where is Roman?
The bastard's abandoned me.
I can't think about that; why does he abandon me
now? The one time. The one time. I have never
abandoned him. I have always been there and he

Darkness

never returns the favour.

My legs begin to buckle.
I've lost control over my body.
Then, the world goes black.

Darkness

Chapter 7

I've always found the darkness to be comforting.
That's why the vividness of the colours perturbs
me. I know this isn't real. It can't be. It
can't be because there is a woman staring at me
and I pretty sure I know her.
I think she's my mum.
She has to be my mum. I don't really remember
the specifics of her appearance or the sound of
her voice. How can I not remember those things?
I wasn't a baby when they pissed off and left me
so why can't I remember?
I want to remember my mum. I hate her for
abandoning me but I want to remembering the
sound of her voice and the scent of her musk,
the thing other kids remember. I want to know
why. I just want to see her in the flesh and

Darkness

here she is. Glowing in the light.

She looks just like me, I guess she would. I have her eyes, her piercing green eyes. The thing is her eyes are too piercing, the green too vivid. Her hair is cropped and blonde, a platinum blonde that overwhelms me. She is beautiful. However, this is how I want her to look; I don't remember her face. I don't remember his face. This is how I want her to be but...she can't be like that. She's worm meat now.

"It's okay, darling. I'm here. Come to me darling. Let go; it's okay baby, let go." Her voice is like a chime, resounding in my head. She looks and sounds angelic.
Let go? Let go of what? Life?
Maybe I should give up. What is the point in living in this craphole? Nothing is ever going to get better. Even if a vaccine was possible, so many people have died that it would seem redundant. I don't want to live in this and I'm tired of fighting; maybe it's my time.

"Mum?"
"Yes baby, I'm here. Come with me, let go."
"I'm scared."
"There's nothing to be frightened of. I'm here, my love. Just come to me."

Darkness

I don't know what to do. Is this what I'm meant
to do? My end game. Kill an infected and die by
a bullet. Alone. Always alone in the darkness.
I could be free. I want to be free.
I'm ready to say goodbye. To the bloodshed. To
Rita. To Roman. To John...
How can I leave him? He's been like a father to
me and he's already lost so much. This is my
choice. I can't hold on for him or anyone.

"I'm ready. I want to come with you."
She just smiles at me and extends her hand. I
walk forward to take her hand. I want this; I
want this.
My fingertips are just inches away from hers
when everything changes. A bright light appears
to burst. It dazes me. Is this the literal light
at the end?
"Elektra. Elektra, look at me! Oh god, you're
bleeding so much. It's going to be okay just
stay with me. Please!"
Roman? I can hear his voice. How can I hear his
voice? I'm dying; do I have a choice?
He's pleading with me to stay but can I really?
He didn't abandon me. I'm scared. I'm
conflicted. My mum is beckoning me to the great
beyond and Roman is pleading with me to stay.

"Elektra, it's alright goose. You're going to be
fine, I swear. Please don't die on us. Rita, can
you stem the bleeding?"

Darkness

"John, I'm trying but I don't think I can. The
bullet has torn a hole in her intestines. I
don't know if there is anything I can do. John,
Roman, now might be the time to say goodbye."
"No, Rita. We can't lose her. Elektra, listen,
if you can hear me please keep fighting, I can't
lose you."
Roman's starting to snivel over me already. Why
are they begging me to stay? I can't. I want to
die but this is heart-breaking. Usually it would
sicken me to my stomach but these are people
that I care about. People that care whether I
live or die. Do I really have the right to die?
After everything with Isla?

Uh, why is this so difficult?
Why did their voices have to penetrate the
bubble around my mind as the bullet pierced my
flesh?
"I need to stitch the hole in the large
intestine but I can't see anything. There's too
much blood, I can't see a damn thing. John,
please accept..."
"No Rita, I am not losing her as well. Stitch
her up or I do it myself. She's a fighter, she
can make it. She'll be pissed at you when she
wakes up and discovers you gave up on her. Do
what you have to do. I need some air, Roman? You
coming with, I need to talk to you."
"But...I want to stay here, in case something
happens. I should have been there, John.

Darkness

I...I..should have been in the haunt with her.
She wouldn't of got hurt. It's my fault."
Roman begins to hyperventilate. There's
something about his cry that gets to me; a
desperate futile yearning. That's the second
time in two days that he's cried. Are they sure
I'm the girl?

I hesitate. My mother waits in front of me,
still smiling radiantly. How can I make a choice
between life and death? I'm needed here. There's
something I heard in all of their voices. Love.
John loves me as a daughter and Roman...Roman
loves me in another way entirely. I should have
seen it before; he's not discreet and he does
love me as more than a friend. Maybe I feel the
same. I mean I have always cared about him. He
is an annoying dickhead but I would be
devastated without him in my life. Not that I
will ever tell him that if I ever wake up. What
am I saying?

Do I pick a certain, a promise of a violent life
surrounded by love or do I pick the unknown? The
end of everything. If death is the end, I am
surrendering to the eternal darkness.

Maybe I don't have a choice.
Death or life?
Is there really any competition between them?
Are they really the same thing?

Darkness

Suddenly, I can feel again. The pain begins to rip through my body. It feels like I'm being ripped apart. I can't do anything. I can't move. I can't scream. I'm trapped inside of my head. I can feel Roman holding onto my hand. His hands are clammy and sticky. It must be my blood I can feel on his hand. He must have found me and carried me back.
If I could just move my hand, it might give him hope. I think he realises how futile it is pleading to me. Uh, why can't I control my own body?
Am I paralysed?
If I am, my decision has already been made. If I'm not, the choice is still there.

Mum still stands here; looking at me. I am ready to do either.
I can feel Roman letting go of my hand. He must have moved because I can feel him kiss my forehead. I can hear his footsteps leave the room.

I'm ready.
"I love you mum."
"I love you too, baby. Let go. Come with me. Freedom, you deserve it baby"
"But...I can't do this."
I take out the blade in my belt. I thrust the blade into her stomach. A blinding ray of light consumes me.

Darkness

I'm not ready to die. I have so much to live for. I want to live, should my body permit it.

I focus everything on moving. The pain is searing through me but I can't think about it. The time for giving up has past. I can find the strength.
I have been so stupid; of course I have something to fight and fight for. I will never stop fighting to live.

"Elektra, sweetheart, can you hear me? If you can hear me, squeeze my hand. Please squeeze my hand. I don't know what else to do. Sweetie, do something."

Rita, I can hear you. I can hear you. I can hear you! I can hear you! I am screaming. I am trapped in my own mind. My own consciousness is fighting me, trying to subdue me. I break through. My heart is still beating and I am still breathing. I can break out of my own mind.

Rita takes my pulse. Her hands must be covered in blood. My blood. She gives a sigh of relief. I guess I am still alive after everything.

"You're a tough girl, you know that. People have died from less. You're not going to give up are you, honey?" She strokes my head "Beautiful girl, it's going to be alright, hey? Keep fighting okay?"

Rita always saw me as an apprentice. I never thought I'd be under her blade again. After getting stabbed in the back and a broken leg, it never had the potential to be fatal. I was conscious the whole time. There was also a greater availability of valid pain medication. I would kill for paracetamol or morphine. Morphine. Anything to take away the pain. Oh god, this is tearing me apart. I can't even ask for it. I just have to open my eyes. Blink. Anything. That's all they need.
I can do something so simple. I can give them hope that they are not wasting drugs.

I will not die.
I will not die.

I feel like there is a barrier. Keeping me from my mobility.
I feel like I am attacking it with a pick axe, trying to escape from the darkness. Adrenaline is pumping through my veins yet again. Natural, not synthetic. That's the only thing keeping my heart pumping.

Adrenaline and rage are a dangerous combination. The barrier is a brick wall. I just keep hitting and hitting and hitting it. It seems strong but

Darkness

I am a stubborn little bitch.
The foundations become weaker and I can see the
first cracks. My eyes are watering so much I
cannot see anything but I keep going. I can't
stop for anything.

Again and again. I will win.
I will not be beaten by my own body.
Suddenly, the first brick begins to fall. It's
not long before the wall begins to crumble. Ha,
brick after brick seems to float into the abyss.
I begin to tear the rest apart with my bare
hands. My hands are becoming bloodier and
bloodier. My fingernails begin to rip off but I
can't think about it. All I can think about is
destroying my Berlin wall.

I've knocked it down. I can see the light. I
keep running and running to the light. I am so
close. Just a little further and then...who the
hell knows what? Do I die after everything? Or
do I wake up? Do I live to fight another day?

I've made it.
One more step and then...it's go time.
I'm ready. Oh, I'm coming for you, you bastards.
I will not be beaten by this. Just one more
step. One more step. Everything will be fine,
why worry?

I step forward and am consumed by the light.

Darkness

Chapter 8

"Welcome back, honey. John, John! Woah, take it easy you've sustained massive internal trauma." The light burns my eyes. I did it. I opened my eyes. I blinked. I'm awake.
Roman is the first to rush through the door; he's like an excitable puppy. He just looks at me in shock. I'm not sure if he's going to cry or faint or both. I'm still trying to find my voice but I can still open my eyes and I can move. I daren't try to get up without incurring Rita's wrath. I am still in discomfort but that's good. Discomfort means I'm alive. My victim is not my murdered, even though the irony would be overwhelming. It would be fitting.

"Hey Ellie, you're looking radiant. Don't ever do that again; I thought I was going to lose you, " he bends down to hug me "Don't ever die okay."
I hug him back. The pain is torture but I don't care. I am loved. What a gratifying thought.

Darkness

He pulls back and just stares at me. His stare
is intense, so intense he seems to be analysing
me. But then again, I'm analysing him. His eyes
are red from crying and there is the reminisce
of snot on the top of his nose. There is also a
red mark on his cheek; it looks like he's been
slapped. I wonder if it was John that walloped
him when it was my fault for leaving him.

I don't want him to let go. How can my opinion
of him alter so drastically in a matter of
moments? Maybe the others were right with their
distorted views of an 'apple pie' life in these
times. That may Roman and I were meant to be.
Am I in love with him or the idea of him? It's
not important anyway, I need time to understand
what I'm feeling. Maybe something will come of
it or maybe not. I don't know if I could even
involve someone in my life in that degree. It's
difficult enough when friend after friend
perishes but a lover dying...I don't know how I
would cope with that.

"You scared us all. John buggered off and no one
has seen him. Erin went to see if she could find
him. A bit of good news at last; turns out you
are a little ray of sunshine miss invincible."
My eyes have to do any form of communicating
because my vocal chords are out of bounds. There
are so many things I want to say: I want to say
I'm sorry that I left Roman after he fainted;

Darkness

I'm sorry that I contemplated dying and I'm sorry for being a weak, pathetic, detached little bitch with delusions of absent strength. But now...now I get to make up for it in some regards.

" Elektra, I'm going to give you some morphine for the pain and some Valerian to help you sleep. Do you understand what I'm saying? Squeeze Roman's arm if you can understand." I squeeze his arm without thinking about it. Drugs. I need drugs.

John used to tell me about the way drugs were moderated; growing herbs like cannabis was prohibited and making drugs such as cocaine and various opiates was illegal. John told me how his unit waged full on war on the UK drug trade. He said he won but then again, he would say that. He was a cop.

Thank god for poppy cultivation. Rita injects me with the newly extracted morphine; it takes a while to take effect but once it does, I feel somewhat peaceful. The pain in my abdomen begins to subside and make way for other sensations. Sensations like hunger, I am absolutely starving, and the sensation that I have to pee. Great, I'm famished and I'm at risk of pissing myself. It just gets better and better I swear.

However, at this moment in time, I am just
relieved at the distinct lack of pain. The pain
spread through my bloodstream like a venom, a
fire that never subsides. But, I don't want to
sleep. After the whole debacle, I don't really
want to close my eyes as I'm scared that I won't
open them again. Rita still hasn't told me what
she's done to fix me up which worries me. I was
like an apprentice, I can take whatever she has
to say. Why wouldn't she tell me when I woke up?
Why?
Calm down Elektra, you're being paranoid. Oh
god, am I talking to myself now? That's when you
know things are going downhill when you find the
only adequate company and reassurance comes from
yourself. Oh lord, this is only going to get
worse. I see it now. Insanity. Straitjacket. Me.
Padded cell. Ah.
Uh, I need to talk to someone. Anyone. I'll take
talking to an animal at this rate. Am I insane?
Or bored? Or both?

Uh, maybe I need sleep or rest. I have just
nearly shuffled off of this mortal coil. I think
I deserve a few hours of peace before everything
begins again. Is it strange that I still don't
want Roman to leave? I just want my bloody
Valerian. It'll look better in the morning. If I
can survive the rest of the day, I will make it.
I am tired. Tired, hungry and bursting for a
piss. Yeah, greatest combination available.

Darkness

I can hear Rita grinding the roots in the old
pestle and mortar. I just focus on my breathing.
In for 5... out for 7. Roman has pulled up a
chair by my head and just sits, stroking my
head. Usually, I'd bash him for even thinking
about touching me but I can do with the comfort.
In for 5...out for 7. The last time someone
stroked my head was so long ago I can't
remember. I tend to bite people when they get
close.

"Okay, just chew the paste and you'll begin to
feel sleepy. What am I going on about, you know
the drill don't you? It's all going to be
alright now. As long as you stay still and don't
rip your stitches. Not that that will happen."

I open my mouth and begin to chew. I've always
hated the taste of Valerian. I've only taken it
when it was absolutely necessary. I went through
an insomniac phase when I was about twelve years
old. It's all that I could do not to go insane
through sleep deprivation.

"I'd better go and make myself useful. Sleep
tight Ellie."
He bends down to kiss my head again and I grab
hold of his arm. He was about to flinch,
whenever I've grabbed him before it's usually
been to inflict pain. But now, I think he can

see what I want to say in my eyes.
Please don't leave.

"It's okay Ellie; if you want me to stay I will.
God, if near death experiences make you so
affectionate, I should have tried this years
ago. Spare years of animosity hey, angel?"
A smile creeps on my lips. Only he can make me
smile at a time like this.

However if he does try to kill me in the future,
I will not be responsible for my actions. As if
he would dare.

He moves his chair around and keeps a hold of my
hand. His hands are still clammy. If I could
talk, I would tell him to wipe his hands or
something. I can't complain though, even if I
wanted too. It's my fault. I can see that his
hands are still covered in my blood. He just
keeps looking at me intensely, as if holding
onto me was a way to keep him alive; letting go
would lead to his demise.

My vision starts to become extremely hazy,
making it difficult to define anything
whatsoever.

A sure sign of my impending slumber.
Everything looks so pretty when nothing is in
focus. It hurts my eyes to keep them open but I

Darkness

want to. No definition. No edges. The colours
seem to blend into each other. Temporary miosis.

I must have relinquished my grip on his hand
because Roman begins to squeeze my hand even
tighter to compensate. It's nice to feel his
presence. Roman is a man of his word so he won't
leave. At least, not until I'm in a deep enough
sleep for him to leave unnoticed.
I think I've caused more than enough chaos and
disruption for one day. Ha, more action have I
brought today than has been seen in years. Can't
accuse the end of days of being boring or
stagnant.

Ugh, I'm getting so tired but I just want to
hold on a tiny bit longer. Why am I fighting
sleep? I shall answer that now. Darkness is no
longer a safe haven for me. The colours and
vibrancy of life far shadow the darkness of
isolation and fear.

I want to relish in the blurred and smudged
colours.
The off white walls blurring into the emerald
shades of the light shade. The grey of the sky
blending into a barren horizon. The peach tones
of Roman's complexion blending into the dark of
his hair.

Darkness

Life, when you think about it, is beautiful. The way water rushes down it's course, undeterred by circumstance or time. The way the birds sing. The way the blades of grass seem to sing on a summer's day. The way life continues after the worst catastrophe.
Survival is the most precious and heavenly.

Oh god, I am becoming delusional. I'm drugged up. I have the right to be completely out of my mind. Ha. I've survived more than I could have anticipated. Bitches can come at me if they think they can but they have to be prepared to shed blood for the privilege.

I just have to...close...my...eyes...

Darkness

Chapter 9

Pain shocks me back into consciousness. I must have rolled onto my side, leaning on my wound. Ow...ow. I should be okay; if I'd have done real damage, it would have hurt even more. I must have winced involuntarily because Rita comes through with another needle. I'm getting sick of my internal monologue; I need to communicate. It's difficult to comprehend how frustrating not being able to communicate is. I'm a solitary creature but even I talk, even if it's to the paintings on the walls in the flat or myself.

"Are you okay? No pain or anything? It's going

to be sore for a good while yet. The bullet did
a lot of damage, honey. I am just going to give
you another shot of morphine to prevent any
discomfort for the moment. I can't believe you
survived; can you speak yet? It's okay if you
can't, the shock can do that but can you talk?"

I have no idea if I can. I could try. Wait.
Shock? I'm not in shock at the moment. If I was
in shock, I wouldn't have felt the pain that
feels like it is killing me. I'm not in shock,
I'm just verbally challenged at the current
time.
"Y...ea..h. Yeah, ah voice. Yeah.
Ow...everything hurts. So if you could hurry and
give me the morphine, that would
be...urgh...wonderful."
Oh yes, I have my voice back. My throat stings
and feels blocked, as if there is catarrh
occupying the inside of my throat but at least
it's back.
Rita quickly fiddles with the needle to get the
dosage right and injects it into my neck. I
think I've been jabbed with a needle so many
times, I've become immune to the initial pin
prick. The relief is what I want; maybe if I
focus on it, it will make it release faster.

The pain begins to subside again. It's still
there, nagging me.

Darkness

The rest of the day passes by very slowly. Rita kept coming in to check on me; she told me it will be at least a month before I can go back to the flat. It will be a fortnight before she would even consider allowing me to walk. Oh, it's going to be a long month. I could really have done without being incapacitated for the short term.

Bloody Roman. Getting me involved with the group again. If you really go into this, this goes back to God. God created the Earth and human beings. He created the virus. He wiped out the population. He created Annie. Annie broke her leg on Earth. Roman came to get help from me. I fix her up. I get shot. I kill a man. That is one hell of a snowball effect. That's only if you really go into it and well...I've got nothing but time at the moment. I'm putting the world's problems on a AWOL cloud deity. Maybe I should stop using he...it's name? Force of habit. Habit. Get it? Nuns, habits?

Am I really making nun jokes? Kill me now; it's a steep path that I have begun to travel. What next, making food puns? Orange you glad I didn't say another nun pun? I haddock no idea? Or my personal favourite, the greatest nut Meg ever knew met a grater.

You're probably wondering where I developed my

wonderful punny humour from. I read them in a
book once; I think it was one of the books I
brought with me when I was found. I sometimes
wonder what type of a kid I was, before meeting
John. From what I gather, I'd never seen a gun
or used a knife. I was so oblivious. I guess
that's something you can say in my parents;
defence; they wanted their child to be a child.
They'd never made me kill anyone or even
understand death. John used to call me his
little 'clueless goose' ,hence my nickname
began. He also called me a little 'savage' but
that's another tale.

I think I would miss being a child if I could
remember a damn thing about it.

I don't know what happened to that book. Maybe
it's still in my room, buried underneath ten
years' worth of clutter. I mean my tastes have
changed over the years; I am nearly twenty years
old. The items in the room have always changed,
like the seasons, from books to guns and dolls
to katanas. Maybe the book survived through my
adolescent outbursts and tantrums.
Amazing the things you remember when you're high
on pain medication. I just spent half an hour
giggling at the many puns I was creating. I am
sure Rita thought I had finally lost my grip on
reality. Then again, the only things I've said
to her were all request for drugs so it's not a

Darkness

difficult thing to accept really.

Oh, apparently I peed myself at some point when
I was asleep. That was not too great a surprise.
I haven't peed myself since I was around the age
of...9. I have no dignity left but what's
dignity anyway? I mean who needs dignity when
everyone's going to die eventually, am I right?
My stomach is also completely empty. I must have
brought up at least a gallon of bile or in that
range. I can't eat anything yet because Rita's
scared that it might cause more damage than it's
worth. She's obviously never been so ravenous
that's she beginning to crave the dirt in the
plant pot. Who the hell has a potted plant these
days? What is the point? Decoration? Or
poncification? Ha, new word. Note to self:
poncification, the act of being a poncified
ponce.

Ah, I do make myself laugh. Internal laugh. I'm
not allowed to laugh externally. That causes
movement and movement is...taboo. God forbid I
should be anything but a vegetable for the mean
time. I wouldn't mind so much if this bloody
bench was comfortable. It is a metal table. Have
you ever slept on a comfortable metal table? No?
Neither have I. Neither have I.

Neither Roman or John have come back yet. That's
rude. I asked Roman to stay. Rude, that's all I

have to say on the matter. Ugh god, I'm high.
And bored. But mainly high. Mixed with a whole
lot of bored. There is only so much
entertainment to be found in a cracked wall tile
and a slip of wallpaper that does not align
properly to the other. Oh and not forgetting the
great section of damp on the ceiling, that's the
best part. No wonder everyone's always wheezing
all the time. Not an infected wheeze. Just a
wheeze. That's a funny word, wheeze. It sounds
like someone has shoved whistle and sneeze
together. Is that where it came from? Genius
Elektra strikes again? Words are strange. Who
came up with wheeze? Or plinth? Or
antidisestablishmentarianism? A wheezing plinth
that stands for antidisestablishmentarianism.
Ha, I'm funny. I tell you what, I may be out of
my sodding tree but I am in the best
mood...ever. People should relish in this. It's
the only time they will not be met with Frosty
the Ice Maiden. I am not just okay, I
am...awesome. I'm an awesome little platypus.

I'm beginning to feel sick again. The more
morphine she gives me, the more I need for any
effect and that Valerian knocks me out like some
form of horse tranquilliser. I sometimes wonder
what it would be like to be out under some form
of anaesthetic. The only thing that can be done
is to hope that they pass out from pain or shock
and that they don't wake up to see a scalpel

making an incision to their abdomen. Believe me,
it's happened before. Quite a few times on
reflection.

I can hear the door open and close.
Someone's come in or gone out. It's probably one
of the girls. That's a thought; where the hell
are they? I haven't seen them all day. The kids
are sometimes sent out to the back up bunker if
things look bad but would they have sent them
away. I don't think they would have sent the
five year old, who paints blood patterns and has
never really understood death or loss, out to
the safe house with the others while they go out
looting. Ha, saying it out loud really
emphasises how messed up things are. An infant
can be detached from death and can not be
frightened of blood.

I was born early into things but there are kids,
where this is all they know. I can remember the
days where there was still usable medicine and
some generators still powered various safe
zones. That's one of my only childhood memories.
Sitting, drinking a hot chocolate and staring
out the window, gazing at the first winter
snowfall. I can't remember what my mum or dad
looked like but I can remember one pointless
night of my existence. I need to know what
happened. Something must have happened. I must
have hit my head or something; that's the only

explanation that fits with my lack of childhood
memory retention.

On the upside, my high is coming to an end. On
the downside, the ripping sensation in my guts
is coming back which means that it's time for
another shot. I'm not so high anymore and yet my
clarity has been compromised. Being out of my
tree somehow gives me total clarity and
expression of thought. Call it a lack of
inhibitions or something along those lines.

The footsteps don't sound like they belong to
flat shoes. So, it can't be one of the girls.
Flat ballet pumps or trainers are the only shoes
that John would let them wear. As soon as I got
my flat, I would walk around the flat in a pair
of four inch heels I found. When I say found,
what I really mean is that they were in the
wardrobe in the flat's bedroom and I 'borrowed'
them. Well, they were dead anyway and I don't
think the dead have any use for stilettos. That
would be weird if they did. Just the dead
tottering around in six inch heels like some
rejected comedy involving zombies. Is that they
are called?

I used to read various comic books when I was
younger but they always called the undead
'walkers' or something similar. I think they
were called 'The Walking Dead' or something

along those lines.

Roman always use to tease me about the fact that
I was reading comics about dead people ripping
living people apart and doing loads of messed up
shit while the other girls were out, sitting in
the garden or chatting about 'girl things'. By
girl things, that means boys, make-up or
periods. It's a weird mix, I'll grant it that.
When I was ten or eleven, Roman was the only boy
at the compound. The girls would always
articulate their devotion to get into his pants.
Need I say, most of these girls were younger
than me. If they were older than me, they were
only a year or so older. Shit is messed up.

How messed up is it that girls that haven't even
gone through puberty yet are able to talk about
sex or as they referred to it as allowing the
'basilisk into the chamber of secrets'? I still
think, to this day, shut up talking about what
you don't understand and go back to playing with
your barbies or guns, whichever comes to hand
first. I cringe even thinking about it but then
again, I'm a prude. Always have been and
probably always will be. Oh it's going to be
awkward when it happens eventually. Oh god, lost
my chain or thought. Lost my train of thought.
Ah. Yes. Um, cannibalistic dead people.

I can hear voices more clearly now. It sounds

like Erin, I'd know her dulcet Northern tones anywhere, and Roman out there. Only one person came in. Am I being avoided? Has someone just sat down in the kitchen in silence to avoid socializing with a bitch in a morphine induced high?
I don't whether to be insulted or not. I'm not sure. Still not sure.
Roman walks into the room. He's sweating from what I can see. He's also panting. Has he been...running? I'm not even going to question it. I'm in too much pain and I'm more interested in something else. Something else that should have come to mind earlier. Roman was saying something when he passed out. I want to know what that was. I have my voice so now, I just have to get a moment alone with him. Away from prying ears and eyes. It made him emotional. I have to find out why. I need specifics.

"Hello, glad you decided to grace me with your presence."
"Hey, I was out looking. You know how it pains me to leave you. I just asked Rita to talk to Erin about a few things outside. So...we have time and you've got your voice back. Shall we talk?"
"Yeah, I think we need to. I'm glad you were the one to suggest it. Even though, I warn you now, I really need my morphine dose right about now. Ow."

Darkness

He just stares at me, as if to question me. As
if to say *why are you being so nice to me? Why
do you think we need to talk? Am I about to die.*
I'm not surprised he's confused. He hasn't been
inside my head; I would be blushing so much
blood would be bursting out of my skin. Ew,
that's a disgusting image but you get the point.

"So all that stuff about Isla..."

Chapter 10

Pain.
That's what I can see in his face. Reluctance as well but primarily, pain. He doesn't want to say it but he knows it's too late for silence on the issue.
"It's complicated," he grimaces.
"I can follow Roman."
He takes a deep breath and begins.

"You have to understand. I am a weasel and a scum bag. I'm everything you think of me-" I try to interject but Roman just shoots me a glare. "I know you really hate me. If Isla had hated me, she might still be alive. When you first moved out, I lost a scavenging partner and someone I loved being around, even when you were

Darkness

being a stubborn bitch.
You know I was always close to Isla because in
some ways, we were the same. Both trying to earn
acceptance, both trying to survive and protect
the people we loved. We began to start hanging
out together and going on runs and we got
closer. I started forgetting my feelings towards
you and my feelings for Isla were amplified. She
was only seventeen but she was older than her
years. Mature. I loved her, Elektra. She loved
me. I never even imagined how it would change
me, you know not having my love unrequited. Isla
never judged me.

I did love her. We began to plan a life
together, a typical life surviving everything
together. We even contemplated having kids,
Elektra. How could we do that? We had quite
a...physical relationship. I didn't force her,
believe me when I say this. She was the one who
wanted sex even though she knew what could
happen. I knew what could happen. Yet we both
shagged like rabbits on heat. John had no idea
what was going on, he thought we were just
friends, but I think if he did know, I would
have lost my manhood by now. I thought so many
times about telling him, he'd have to find out
eventually but we were just living for the
moment.

I wanted her. You would pop out every now and

then and I begin to remember that you were still
there. You seem detached as if you needed
someone to be there for you. I would have come
to you this week even if Annie hadn't been hurt;
I missed you and after Isla, I just needed some
form of companionship. Isla was jealous. She
thought that you meant more to me. I reassured
her constantly but she was never convinced. I
should have been with her every moment, not
worrying about your detachment because ,let's
face it ,you have never really been right in the
head. You were born for this world, Ellie.
I am a dickhead. I am a douche bag. I didn't
make her feel as if she was the only girl in my
world but she wasn't.

Isla had been getting sick. John had been
getting worried about her but I guess she knew
exactly what it was. Rita had stock piled
pregnancy tests so I stole one. I was scared but
ecstatic; I was going to be a father. It would
be difficult but I had never been so excited.
John would probably have hung, drawn and
quartered me. When she confirmed it, I was
elated and I swore to protect her and the baby.
She kept talking about sticking a coat hanger up
there and scooping the little ball of cells out;
we fought about it. Our last fight. I guess I
wouldn't have the same reluctance as she would,
I wouldn't have had to push a baby with a twelve
inch head out a one or two inch hole.

Darkness

I wish I'd just relented; whatever happened, the baby wasn't supposed to be born. Maybe it would have been the kindest thing to let her abort the pregnancy but I was too stubborn and pig headed to see beyond my own desire. I have always wanted to be a dad. You think I look after the girls for extra credit with the powers that be but that is not close to the reason. I do it because I love the kids.

After our last fight, she went out on a run. I told her not to, that she could get hurt and that I should go with her but she wouldn't have it. She told me to piss off and that if she wanted to put herself in danger that she would. I should have stopped her. I should have grabbed hold of her or at least, told her that I loved her. When she came back, she wouldn't talk to me or even look at me.
I didn't even know she was sick until Rita told me that Isla was close to death and that she was bleeding heavily. She was miscarrying and dying. Miscarrying and dying. Then, she was dead. She died thinking that I was a possessive dick. She died hating me. It was my fault, she went out to cool off after an argument with me. If I had just relented, she wouldn't have gone out and probably would have miscarried naturally. I wouldn't have lost yet another person I care about.

Darkness

You wanted to know about what happened with
Isla. Now you know Elektra. Now it's time for
you to talk. I've bared my soul, now it's your
turn."

I am in shock. Isla was...pregnant? I cannot
believe the both of them were so reckless and
downright stupid. Ah! How could they be so
stupid?
I should probably have responded with
reassurance like *I don't hate you, you were
right to be persistent because it was your child
too.* But I can't respond like that. I can't
reassure him because whatever I say would never
be enough. He talked about how I was responsible
for some of the conflict with Isla because he
wanted to be there for me. No, he didn't. He
wanted to be more than just 'there for me'. One
of his lamest excuses to date. In essence, he
blames me partly for her death which is not
fair. How was I supposed to know about the
entirety of their bullshit brigade?
Oh and he wants me to talk now?
What the hell does he expect me to talk about?
Does he just want me to spout off pathetic
remarks of sympathy and empathy. I feel
differently about him now but I am still
repulsed by what he, what they, did.
"Elektra?"
I look up.

Darkness

"What do you want me to say Roman? You want sympathy or empathy? You know I'm not the one to go to for that crap. You get your leg up, she was baking a bun in her oven and then she got sick. Is there really anymore to be said?"
He just looks at me as if I killed a puppy. I was asking a question. I'm guessing he wanted some melodramatic performance or an argument but why would I give him that? He can torture himself just fine, he doesn't need by intervention.

"You really don't care about it, do you?" he says dejectedly.
"I do care but it's done. Nothing can be done to change it now, she's dead and gone. You can't take anything back which I see as punishment enough. Plus, I'm still quite mellow from the morphine but that will change soon. What did you want to know?"
" I guess you're right. You didn't have to be such a bitch about it but you're right. I want to know what you really think about me. Why you left me yesterday. Everything."

"What do I really think? I think you are a self righteous dick head with such a little understanding of the world that I'm surprised you're not dead yet. But, I...I...I think you are a decent human being who doesn't deserve the hand he's been dealt and I don't hate you. Far

86

from it. If anything I respect you. That's the truth about it. I left because I was bored and I didn't want to wait for you to wake up."

Bluntness is by far the best method of articulation. I think that's shocked him into silence for a few minutes. It does take his little brain quite along time to process things. Why did I tell him I respected him? He will never let me forget that I said that. I could never tell him I feel anything but respect for him otherwise I would never live that down. Then again, I shouldn't want to live it down should I? If I have any stronger feelings then I should want to tell him but now is not the time, not by any means.

"God. Don't hold back Elektra. You respect me? You. Respect. Me?"
"Oh don't worry, I won't and shut up."
"So you don't hate me? Well, I will admit you give mixed signals. You must be an amazing actress then to keep me in ignorance for so long..."
"I may not be able to get up but I can still strangle you with my shoe laces if you don't shut up."
"Okay, whatever you so Lex"
"Wait, since when have you called me Lex? Nobody calls me Lex; I just about tolerate being called Ellie, but Lex?"

Darkness

In truth, it might grow on me. Lex. A new
nickname long overdue. Lex. Yeah, that might
work for me. I will show disdain when he uses it
but I actually quite like it. But why after all
this time is he electing to call me a new name.
Has he got bored of it or is it now too childish
after nearly dying. I also used to find being
called Ellie patronising because it seemed like
such a youthful name, a name befitting a child
who hasn't witnessed bloodshed. I don't really
think it suits me anymore. I can't be classified
as innocent and I haven't been innocent for a
long time. Maybe Lex is the new me. Someone
baptised in blood and fire. Someone who has
faced death and fought against it. Yeah, Lex is
the new me, a new beginning if you will. Uh, how
melodramatic did that sound? Did those words
genuinely come of out of my mouth.

I guess the saying becomes true; new me, new
rules.

New me, new rules.

Chapter 11

John still hasn't reappeared.
Now I'm starting to get worried. It's been over
a fortnight since he went missing. Over a two
weeks since I got a bullet through the gut.
I'm fine though. I'm being wheened off of the
morphine which means I am in a constant state of
pain at the moment. It's not as bad as when it
first happened. The pain is no longer sharp and
searing but more of a dull ache that won't go
away. If I could compare it to anything I would
compare it to a tooth abscess.

However, I've been told to 'embrace the pain' as
pain is a sign that I'm alive. Roman showed me a
picture of my stitches with John's old polaroid
camera that he keeps locked in his safe box in
his bedroom. I look absolutely brutal even
though I am going to have a beautiful ragged
scar. Rita is brilliant at what she does but she
can't sew stitches for shit. A war ravaged
torso. Rita's hands shake a lot which is why she

Darkness

was training as an apprentice. It is dangerous for her to have so much power over someone's life when her talent is being stolen by arthritis.

Roman and I have been on good terms since our conversation a few days ago; he hasn't really left my side which has been okay. I haven't been as painfully bored as per usual which is great. The more time we spend together, the more I begin to enjoy his company. He knows how to make me laugh, really laugh. I never realised it before but he is genuinely funny. He knows how to make me truly belly laugh, which is incredibly painful as laughing involves abdominal muscle movement. I never really enjoyed his company before because I guess I didn't want to. I didn't want to affiliate with anyone with a pulse...or no pulse. I haven't just gained a necrophiliac tendency. Necrophiliac tendencies, ew.

Even though I've had the company of Roman, the bloody part time comedian, I can't help but worry about John. As far as he's concerned, I'm still on death's doorstep and getting closer to the pearly gates every second. I hope he hasn't done anything stupid. Or reckless. He's not as young as he used to be; his immunity is pretty bad which means he gets illness that goes around. That's why he rarely leaves the base because if he were to be in close proximity to an infected. Please John, don't be dead.

My death could have been the one thing that finally tipped him over the edge. At the end of the day, I could never have allowed myself to die. I genuinely believe that he may have topped himself. If he had killed himself, I would never have been able to forgive myself. Not that I would be able to do anything when I entered the eternal slumber but I still wouldn't be able to cope with that. You know, if there is something beyond life that encompasses some form of being.

"That scar is brutal, fitting for an ice maiden. Brutal but refined. Beautiful like its wearer." He smiles at me as he always does. I begin to blush. I'm not pretty. I don't know how to accept any form of compliment, especially when his hand is so close to my who-ha. He notices my blushing which makes him giggle even more. His giggle makes me giggle. Next thing you know, we're both laughing again. I guess the reason I am so willing to bear my soul to someone is because I need someone. I need solid proof that I am needed . That I have a reason for living and I have not taken the difficult route for no viable reason.

"It still aches, you know. It feels nice having your cold hand on a injury that feels like it is

burning. How massive are your hands?"
"You know what they say. Big hands, big..."
"I don't need you to finish that sentence. Ha, I
thought you were going to say the other saying,
you know 'cold hands, warm heart'."
"That would explain your freakishly warm hands,
ice maiden."
"Ha ha, very funny. It would fit. I hate when
you're right, you dickhead."

We continue to giggle and we we stop, we just
stare at each other. This is awkward. I have
never felt this awkward around him and I think
he can sense it as well. Something changed the
moment that bullet tore through me. It's for the
better in some cases, Roman, but bad in other
cases. At the moment, I am at my most vulnerable
and I'm becoming more emotionally bonded to
people. Damn it. It feels like a better thing,
more human, but it is the kind of thing that
will get me killed, for real this time. A head
injury or something.

"Roman, can you help me with something in here?
You can continue flirting later." I introduce to
Rita, the cock blocker. He grunts. I can't help
but giggle at the way he rolls his eyes and
grunts like a bloody farmyard animal. He smiles.
Roman gets up and leans over to kiss my head,
yet again, and I act on impulse. I lean up and
my lips touch his. We stay like that for a few

seconds, just our lips touching, and then he
backs away. I've shocked him. I've shocked
myself. Did I actually just kiss him?
Yes, I think I did. I kissed Roman. Oh god, I
shouldn't have done it. Played right into his
hands. Uh, I'm screwed. Screwed. Screwed.

"Wait a minute," I hear him say from the
kitchen.
He walks back into the living room and kisses me
again. This time with more...passion. I can't
believe this actually happening. I would blame
it on the morphine is Rita had given me any. I
want this. I actually want this. It seems John
was always right; I was just too stubborn to
even consider it. When he finally breaks away
for air, he just smiles and kisses me on the
nose. I've never been kissed on the nose before.
I don't like it but then again, I have a
ticklish spot on my nose. Who has a ticklish
spot on their nose? In my defence, it is my only
ticklish spot. Well, there and my feet but the
last person who touched my feet ended up dead so
take from that what you will.

He walks into the kitchen again, with a beaming
smile plastered on his face. This must be what
he has wanted for the longest time. The longest
time. If I hadn't of been shot, I would never
have allowed the thought to cross my mind. I
would have spent the rest of my life mindlessly

resenting him due to fear. The way I figure it, I have survived death. Fought it and won. I've done it once, I can do it again. So, death can come at me and take its best shot because I'm stronger than even I know. I have no reason to be frightened of dying anymore. Loss is still a threat but death itself is something I no longer fear because I know I have a choice. I'll always have a choice and I'll always choose life until I can't anymore.

"Miss Milton, good to see you looking so lively."
The dulcet northern tones continues to linger after the last syllable is uttered. Erin. Everyone's favourite ex social worker. She still believes that she still serves a purpose even though what is the point of having someone to safeguard children when they're dropping down like flies? I don't understand but John felt she needed a reason to go on. She feels like she has to protect all of the children because she couldn't protect her own. She lost her son a month into the outbreak and she has never forgiven herself. I think that's why she's always had a soft spot for Roman; they would have been the same age and he could pass for Erin's son. They have the same eyes.

"Erin, I was wondering when you were going to make an appearance to brighten my life. So,

where's my get well present, you bitch?"
She goes bright red; I don't think she
understands the concept of sarcasm. I think
that's why I enjoy tormenting her so much? So
gullible. I've tried the whole 'gullible's
written on the ceiling' and she falls for it
every single time. I shouldn't torment her but I
get so much satisfaction out of it. My way of
taking pain out on others. Oh, I am evil bitch
when I want to be.

"I'm kidding, Erin. Sarcasm. Sarcasm, Erin."
"Oh, yes of course. I'm sorry it took me so
long; I had some business to take care of,
looking for some more flats or places of
accommodation. I've found a lovely little
bungalow if you would like to exchange. There's
more room and it's closer..."
"Thank you, Erin. Yes, if you can sort it out.
The amount of blood and...hm...other bodily
discharges freak me out as I have told you many
times. I want the bungalow...please."
"I know but this bungalow is perfect. Perfect
for you to start off. I was surprised to find
it, it had been ransacked but it is sufficient.
It is perfect for you to settle down. You know,
have children..."
"No," I interrupt " The bungalow would just be a
starting point. Is John with you? Have you seen
him? Did he come with you?"
"No Elektra. I haven't seen him in a while; I

know everyone's worried about him but he can
look after himself. I've seen that man survive
things I 'int thought possible. He'll be fine."

What she says reassures me. She has known him
for twenty one, eleven years longer than I have
so she must know a thing or two. She been there
when he's been through loss and joy. He's been
through a lot, we all have, but he hasn't given
up yet so he'll be fine. I mean, he has to be
otherwise it's not just going to be Rita and I
that are affected. John and Erin, before the
outbreak, had a brief romantic relationship. It
was complicated because Erin had a son and John
had a wife. But it still happened. However, that
the thing about the end of days; it's a bit of a
romance killer especially when death becomes
involved. Recalling old times. That's the reason
he wanted Erin to feel like she had a purpose.
He was protecting her because he knew what grief
could do to a sane person, not built for this
kind of a world. A world where it is dangerous
to cough or sneeze. Where you can't step outside
of the house without being terrified that the
virus may have become air borne overnight. Where
death is common place.

I'm not the only one that John saved from the
flames.

"Rita tells me you should be able to walk about

Darkness

soon. That will nice for you, being mobile
again. Not be trapped in bed."
"Yeah, it will be. I am sick of the sight of
this room. They're planning to shove me in the
garden for a few hours to take my mind off of
things. Is it warm out there? Are they shoving
me out there to give me hypothermia in the hopes
of killing me off?"
"No, they are not trying to kill you to my
knowledge. You don't seem to understand how much
your injury has traumatised people. The younger
children look up to you and Roman. The poster
people of survival. It scared them to know
you're just human."
"Well, we're not invincible. Nobody is and they
need to learn that, Erin. Never let them become
complacent or think anyone is above dying.
Anyone can die. Anyone. Including the 'poster
people'."

I may have come across as harsh but it is the
gospel truth. Nobody is above dying and everyone
does. There is no point in placing faith in
people to live for eternity just because they
have constructed a tougher shell. The moment you
find yourself above death is the moment you
expose your vulnerability. Fate hates
complacency. The kids look up to Roman and I?
Why would they? Roman okay, he protects them and
acts as eye candy for the girls and a role model
for the boys but me? Me? What the hell have I

done to deserve being admired? I'm hardly ever
around. I'm obnoxious, bitchy, sarcastic and
detached, I think that sums me up sufficiently,
so why would kids look at me and think 'damn, I
want to be like her when I grow up'?
That is seriously messed up.

The awkward silence. I don't know how to follow
up my previous comment and Erin is looking at me
as if I have committed genocide. Why do people
keep looking at me as if I am some evil neo-Nazi
who kills puppies? They say the kids look up to
me? The way people look at me would suggest
otherwise. They look at me as if I am some sort
of pariah. Am I a pariah? Maybe I am. Maybe.
However the definition of a pariah is ' a person
who is generally despised or avoided. I am not
avoided. There have been times when I have
desired to be avoided but that never happens;
something always drags me back here. A catch up
or an accident. I can never avoid this place and
I guess, I wouldn't change that for anything.
Maybe I'm not a pariah but I may just be a
virago with a sociopathic nature. That could fit
with me. Plus I like the word 'virago' better
than 'pariah'.

"You are right Elektra. They need to accept that
but I won't be the one to tell them. If you feel
so strongly about it, you tell them. You might
not see yourself as influential but they listen

to you. I'd better go, check on the bungalow.
I'm glad you're okay. It's a miracle you are."
"Fine. You know me Erin, miracle worker- London
division. I do love to defy odds especially when
I'm needed. I'm too loyal for my own good. Too
loyal to die, I guess. Bye."

She opens her mouth as if to say something but
closes it. I don't think she can find anything
to say. I seem to be shocking people a lot
lately, some people for better reasons than
others. But then again, what is a good reason?

She wants me to talk to the kids. She
wants...me...to talk to the kids. Me? Yes, I
feel strongly about it, granted, but I'm not the
only one. She knows talking to the kids is my
own form of torture; having all of those faces,
still full of hope, believing in me and I have
to destroy their faith and scare them. I will
say it again, torture. The sadistic bitch.

Roman waits in the door way, watching Erin leave
out of the back door. He is too nosy for his own
good, he's not stupid. Well, I'm conflicted on
that one; he eavesdrops everything. He's not
stupid but I wouldn't call him the brains of
Britain if you get my drift. He just turns to me
and smiles. I am dreading this moment; now I
have to answer for my actions. Oh god. He is
going to relish in this.

Darkness

"Rita's sent me to come and get you. She's even got the wheelchair out for you, you lucky thing you. You ready, Lex?"
"I am not worthy, I am not worthy. Of the decrepit wheelchair. Yes, I'm guess I'm going to have to be."
"Let me help you up. Get them little feet working."
"Little feet, my feet are bigger than yours. You and your dainty little ballerina feet."
"I'm still growing. My feet are just in a period of stagnation. Ballerina feet. Ballerina feet?"
"A little help please? You know if you don't topple over because you're too tall for your feet; the base not being wide enough."
"I'm going to get you for that."

He comes closer to be and begins to kiss me again. He said Isla was the one who wanted a physical relationship. I finding that to be false but then again, I was never in a relationship with Isla. At least I don't think I was. Alcohol does release inhibitions but that's the curse, you can't remember which inhibitions have been released and onto whom. Ha, I'm kidding. Well, maybe. As I said, alcohol what a bastard. He seems to put more pressure onto my lips as if he is trying to get into my knickers. He is a passionate person anyway but ...whoa. Aye aye. He begins to move his hands from on my face to my chest to my stomach to my... I pull away. I have only just kissed him; god, I'm not a slut. If he wants that then he's got to put a ring on it. I have a feeling I'm going to die a virgin at this rate.

"I'm sorry. I just get so...pent up."
"I know you do, considering you were just about to try and mount me. Wow."
We both look at each other and burst out laughing yet again. Maybe being with Roman will be easier than I anticipated. He still hasn't questioned me which gives me some form of reassurance. I guess he's just satisfied to be able to get that close to me; to be so close to getting into my knickers. Men may deny it but that's the ultimate aim at the end of the day, isn't it? I just go on what I've heard growing up. The many men that have left have only been interested in their next shag. Procreation and all that jazz.

Maybe this is the right thing? To just take things slowly with Roman? Just getting to know him for who he truly is?

I'm prepared.

Chapter 12

For the first time ever, it's not actually
raining. It's warm. I know that is definitive
proof it's the end. Sun in England, who have
thought it? The wheelchair isn't exactly
comfortable and stinks of vomit but it serves a
purpose. Getting into it was difficult. My legs
were numb after spending two weeks not being
allowed to move so even moving an inch is pretty
much impossible. I feel like I have undergone
temporary paralysis in my legs, my only
salvation is that Rita has shoved a pin in my
foot many times which has made me react. A sign
that I am not paralysed.

Roman had to lift me. By the waist. Where my

scar is. You can imagine how that went down.
It's all fun and games until someone touches the
scar, then all hell breaks loose. The pain was
pretty bad but I played it up, giving Roman the
guilt trip of a lifetime. I think I convinced
him I was dying again. I still get so much
pleasure bedevilling his ass. I should probably
stop...Nah.

Once I finally got into the chair, the smell
made me gag. How many people have puked up onto
the chair? How do you do that anyway, when you
are actually in the chair?Do you part your legs
and then just release the contents of your
stomach? It smells so bad, so bad. It's vile, on
the verge of setting off my gag reflex which
when unable to escape from the aforementioned
smell, you can imagine. I understand such items
as wheelchairs are a rarity, I understand that,
but really? Can you not replace it? I don't
know, get a chair and attach wheels to it. I
can't be the only one that is bothered by it.
When they're not trying to give me hypothermia,
they're trying to make me vomit my damaged
organs up through my mouth.

Rita was saying, earlier, how my intestines did
suffer quite severe damage that may 'cause
discomfort' for a while. The organs' functions
may be impaired which means there is still the
chance of an internal infection. C'est

magnifique. Oh the irony; surviving the initial impact to die because of my body fighting against me. I'll be fine; I always am. I've been eating and everything seems to be in order which is a positive sign. However, I have to face that possibility. My body can turn on me at any time. I was shot with a magnum for god's sake. I'm lucky I didn't have a chunk blown out of me. I'm lucky I didn't die right then and there. Carpe diem, right?

The landscape is fairly minimal but I finally have the distraction I've been looking for. The garden is relatively small in comparison to the dimensions of the house. Yes, I don't think this place is going to be looking like Old McDonald's farm anytime soon. The garden's borders are marked by a large wooden fence which makes the garden seem like a corridor. When there is the rare occasion of a warm day, it seems somewhat darker than it should. It's been painted white so that helps reflect some of the light and heat but it is still a minimal amount. The grass is well maintained but then again, John always was fond of a garden he could be proud of. During the warm days, he would have all of us out in the garden tending to the it. Cutting the grass, dealing with the weeds, tending to the vegetable patch. Ah, the infamous vegetable patch.

John was so determined to make that patch work.

Darkness

A natural supply of food; living off of 'the
fatta the land', if you'll pardon the Steinbeck
quote. He had everyone out in force, planting
and maintaining these little cabbage, carrot and
pea plants. I was about thirteen at the time. I
went through a kind of existential crisis at
that point. Everyone does; what is the point in
living? I'm an insignificant little blip on the
grand scheme of things, I can be irradicated
without any repercusions. Yeah, we all have that
thought at least once and if you haven't, you
are lying through your teeth. Anyway, tending to
this garden, this insignifcant item that could
go on to do things bigger than itself. What I
mean is that one of those plants could feed a
person that would go on to change the world,
conquer the virus. They could give someone the
strength to survive. Shame they could keep up
their end of the bargain.
If you're wondering what happened to the plants,
if you are so enamoured with the story of the
vegetables, they may have been drowned. By
accident. They may have been trodden on too.
Well, I say trodden, I mean stamped on. Fire may
have been involved but that's not important.
John never found out the assailant. The
assailant who murdered his poor little plants.
Oh how my heart breaks for those poor
minute...vegetables.

I really have needed fresh air. There is

something liberating about being outside. I can't exactly run away or do anything but appreciate things. I've felt so stiffled lately; the air seemed to be becoming heavier, pressing down on my lungs and suffocating me. I feel like I can breathe again. I can breathe again. I'm surprised the kids aren't out here but from what I can tell, they've been sent out to try and find John. I should be out there, looking for him, but I'm pretty bloody useless being incapacitated. I just feel...so incompetent. Everyone's been out there...everyone but me and it's my fault that he left, I think.

It's Spring. It must be either April or May, it's always difficult to tell. No watches, no calendars. Time is really no object anymore. It could be one of three months; the seasons seem to fuse and merge. Spring is one month that fuses into summer and then that fuses into autumn ending with the death of life and vibrancy in winter. It feels so asinine. The seasons are months, clumps of weather patterns and changes. You could relate the seasons to life; spring being birth; summer being the peak of life and a person's vibancy; autumn representing later life and the disintegration of everything. Then comes winter which robs everything. Ability, love, life. Winter is the end of days, a profound thought. Ah, seasons being a metaphor for life, how cliche. But, it's

Darkness

undeniably true.

I always hated the spring. Spring, the season of
perpetual rainful and romance. It was sickening.
I always prefered the autumn. It always seemed
more...refreshing. The beginnings of the cold,
gripping onto life and forcing into submission.
I prefer it because it's not too hot, not too
cold. Just perfect. Also, there is something
quite relaxing about watching something so
immortal succumb to the will of the planet.
Nature versus the ideas of science. Space versus
nature.

Roman steps out of the kitchen to join me.
He pulls up an old deckchair and places it next
to me and just links his hand with mine.
We just sit in silence for a while. For seconds,
minutes, hours. He can sense that I just need to
be alone with my thoughts. When I become
engrossed in my thoughts, nothing else seems to
matter anymore. All I can think about is John.
If he's okay. If the kids are okay. I have to
know if he is safe, it's like torture to be in
ignorance. Is this what it was like before? When
I was waiting for my parents to come home? Did I
yearn for them like I yearn for John's return
now? Is there really anything more to say?

There is no way to break the silence. I can't
help it. My eyes begin tearing up; I am too

tired to stop myself. I think Roman and I have
overcome that barrier, I mean I've kissed him
now. I guess he can see that I am human, not the
detached little soldier he thinks I am. How can
I be a soldier? The war's already been lost. I
just let the tears rush down my face. What's the
point in keeping a false pretence? I've seen
Roman at his weakeast and he's now seen me at
mine. I can't be strong anymore.

He looks over at me. He has no idea what to do.
I can't stop the tears but I don't even know
what I'm crying about. John? The fact that I
killed a man in cold blood? The pain that
courses through my venom like an inferno?
Roman gets up from his chair. He's going inside;
even he can't handle female emotions. That might
be another reason, I'm just being an over
emotional female. But he does something that I
have not anticipated. He bends down and picks me
up, out of the chair. The ache in my abdomen
starts again but I can't bring myself to care. I
am bloody useless, incompetent. He then sits
down on the deck chair, with me in his arms, and
just rocks me. I snuggle into him. I just need
someone to be there for me right now. I need
someone to understand.

«It's okay baby, let it go. It's alright, I'm
here. It's going to be alright.»
That's when I break. Great, ugly sobs are

released from deep with in my chest. The amount of saliva, tears and snot on Roman's shirt is quite impressive, I must say. He doesn't seem to care. He just keeps rocking me and comforting me. How have I been so wrong about someone for so long ? He's a decent man who I really do not deserve. The things I've done ; the things I can forget.

We stay like this for hours. I continue to snuggle into Roman, it's getting a lot colder and the shivering is only making it worse. I just need to calm down; reclaim use of my own lungs when grief is threatening to steal them.
«Are you cold?»
I nod, unable to utter a syllable for fear that when I open my mouth, nothing will come out. He moves me slightly forward and takes his jacket off. He then places the jacket around my shoulders and brings me further in, placing his arms around me like a protective barrier.
«Thank you,» I whisper. I think he heard me because he smiles.

I just want to sleep. It's right what they say, crying is exhausting. I feel emotionally exhausted but I don't want to leave the comfort of Roman's arms. For the first time in a while, I feel safe. Secure. I don't want this moment to end.

Darkness

Roman is still awake, stroking my hair and gazing into the distance. He's here. He's not exactly going anywhere at the moment. I allow myself to succumb to sleep.

I am sure of only one thing. I cannot lose Roman. I won't let that happen.

I'm going to start by finding John.

Darkness

Chapter 13

I wake up to the feel of rain piercing through
my flesh. Roman still has his arms wrapped
around me but he must have fallen asleep hours
ago. Falling asleep in each other's arms, how
sickeningly punctilious. My injury feels like a
dull ache but the ache in my head is
preoccupying most of my attention. Ow, my head.
I also get the mother of all headaches after I
cry; it wouldn't surprise me if I get a
migraine. Fantastic. Incapacitated and blind to
the world.

My mind is set. I know what I have to do. I have
to find John and, although it may be painful and

Darkness

slow, I can move. Now is my perfect opportunity.
It's pitch black. Roman is snoring away like a
baby warthog. The lights are all out inside the
house. It's now or never. If I don't go now,
they won't let me. I just have to hope that I
don't wake Roman when I wiggle my way out of his
grip.

I can't help feeling nervous; wouldn't Roman
come with me if I woke him up? Would he shop me
in to the others? I can find him, I know I can.
I move slowly, trying to use as little energy or
force as is possible. It's like attempting to a
limbo. Once I have escaped his grip, I land on
the grass with a little thump. That was loud,
loud enough to wake him up. He will have felt
that.
Shit.

I can't get up. My legs are so stiff due to the
lack of blood circulation. I'm not sure I can
actually get up; my plan was stupid. My plan
relied on me being in anyway mobile. I can't
believe I could be so moronic. Uh! I might be
able to crawl. If I can crawl, that might get
the blood flowing back into my legs. I have had
two weeks of not using them, obviously there's
going to be an issue with using them when I
desire. Damn it.

I look up to see if Roman is still asleep. Yes.

Darkness

Then again, that man could sleep through a
hurricane so take from that what you will. He is
no longer what I have to worry about. I crawl
forward a few meters. Downside, everything is
killing me; upside the blood's flow in my legs
seems to be coming back. I place my arms on the
wheelchair. The smell of vomit and piss hits me
instantly. Piss is the new flavour, ew. I could
gag. I could gag. I just have to push myself up.
I have good abdominal strength; I could pull
myself up easily, usually. However, these are
not the usual circumstances. I just have to
focus all of my energy and strength into my
arms.

Ha. I'm doing it. My legs are threatening to
buckle but I'm determined. I'm doing it. I've
done it. I'm standing. Whether I can move is
another thing entirely. One step could cause me
to topple which is the worst thing possible. I
just need to hold onto the chair. I put one foot
in front of the other. I stamp my foot; the
grass masks the sounds but Roman still fidgets.
He fidgets and crosses his arms, moving to sleep
on his right side. He drags his legs up to his
chest. He's in too deep in sleep to notice my
absence; this is a good thing for me. This is
okay.

My feet still feel numb. So numb, they don't
feel like they're there. They don't feel like

113

their belong to me. Walking. It should be just
like riding a bike. I can't feel where my feet
are which makes me feel like I am about to fall
any second. I just have to leg it. Run and if I
fall, I fall. I have to try. I run. I'm running
like Bambi on ice; my legs feel like they are
flailing which is a bloody weird sensation but
I'm moving. I just have to open the back gate
and I'm on the home stretch. I twist and pull
the lock. The lock is rusted and archaic; it's a
bit tough but I can still pull it free. It's
like a natural child lock. I push the gate; now,
I have time to find him.

It feels as if I have killer stomach cramps.
Maybe I do. What a perfect time to start. Or
that might be the intestines shouting out. I'm
still not healed and there may be an infection.
Rita's put me on some form of antibiotics but it
isn't possible to know if they will work.
Antibiotic resistance is a bitch. I have this
one opportunity. They will probably shit a brick
when they find me gone; I've already terrified
Roman with my near death experience. Ever since
I woke up, he's always been there watching over
me. I don't really want to do this to them again
but...I have to find John. I feel a sense of
loyalty and duty to him. He's always found me
when I was lost.

The alleyway is pitch black. A few years ago,

Darkness

the street lamps were still functional; there
was something more confrontational because you
could see shadows in every direction. The light
seemed to illuminate everything, I guess that's
why I prefer the darkness. Ignorance is bliss
after all.

I walk slowly.
Every inch of my body feels like it's been
bruised. I have to limp to walk; why? I have no
idea whatsoever. I have a goal now; I have to
focus on that now. It is so quiet. It's always
peaceful but this is eerie. This is what it
would be like to be the last human being
standing; my footsteps and birdsong. The only
sounds left. And the rain. Can't forget the
rain. The sound of rain. The haunting
combination of bird song and rain.

I've sometimes wondered who would survive, who
would be the last human on Earth. There's no way
to know how many people are still out there.
There could be thousands out there, unaffected
by the contagion. African nations where energy
was not a problem. Places in the Himalayas or
other mountainous regions where the air is
clear. I believe there are still whole countries
that weren't infected, where millions of people
are still thriving. I know there are others out
there, I mean there have to be.
I've always wanted to travel and see if there is

hope. I was planning to go on an 'excursion'
when Roman turned up. I was going to finally do
it. Something always got in the way but I have a
plan now.
I find John, make sure he's okay. Then I collect
a sufficient amount of supplies and I get some
form of transportation, like a bicycle. Then, I
hit the road. I know it would take weeks to get
to Scotland or Wales but it will be worth it.
They are my best bet. Travelling anywhere else
would require water transport. Preferably a boat
and without petrol, I would be looking at a
little sail boat which would be totally useless.

Maybe I would take someone with me. I guess I
have to. I would have to take Roman with me. I
guess the real question is: do I want to? I
mean, I do feel more than just friendly
affection for him but I've always felt that this
was my mission. My end game. This was my
formulation and would he ever want to leave the
camp, where he has a purpose and where he
belongs? This always felt like I had to do this
alone.

Anyway, I have to focus on this. I have had that
plan formulating in my head for years. I've
spent month upon month thinking about my plan of
action. I still have time. Time to focus on that
once I know that John is in good health.

Darkness

I need to think. I mean I've just gone AWOL, I
have to be totally sure that what I'm doing will
yield results. I have to be sure that I will
find John. There has to be a place he would go;
it's been over two weeks so he can't be too
exposed meaning he must have found some form of
safe house.
Come on Elektra, think. Think. He must have
mentioned something to me. There must be
somewhere. Somewhere he mentioned that he would
go. Come on, come on.

I've got it.
I know where he's gone..
The others would never have thought of it; why
would they?
Where would anyone go when they're lost or
frightened?
Home; he's gone home.

John took me there a few years ago. It had been
pillaged and there had been a death there but it
was his home before everything. He'd gone there
to find some form of solace. I still don't know
why he took me, he should have taken Isla. But,
he took me. He must have felt like I may need to
know it one day. How right he was, if that was
his thought process at the time.

There were still pictures there. The only thing
of his that was still there. That the thing

about scavengers, they don't tend to still
family photographs. Even they aren't so callous.
I remember looking at this one photo, it must
have been a wedding photo. I'll admit it, he was
handsome. He had these blonde curls and was
cleanly shaven. It was strange seeing him like
that, all dressed up in a tuxedo with a grin
plastered onto his face, but the eyes lead to
the ease of identification. His grey eyes.
Staring into the soul, showing an understanding
beyond words. He has his arm around his bride.
She looked radiant with he auburn hair flowing
in the breeze. Her chocolate brown eyes were
gazing into his grey eyes. Such different eyes
expressing one sentiment. Love. She was quite
pretty but I would put that down to the
excessive make up. Her nose seemed to be crooked
and beak like but her eyes were...cute. Wide and
alert like a baby barn owl. They made an
attractive couple; I don't understand why their
relationship didn't work but then again,
pictures can be deceptive. It is easy to stage a
picture but real life, not so much. But at that
moment, love seemed to radiate from them,
through the image.

John just sat staring at this one picture. Just
that one. I peered over his shoulder trying to
get just a glimpse of it and that I did. The
image was unclear. It was black and white making
me think it was an older picture but it couldn't

be. The date at the bottom said: '17th February, 2003' and it said '16 weeks' in a white marker pen. It's not exactly recent but there still had coloured images because the wedding photo had the date of the '25th December, 1996'. John would have been twenty one years old. That's strange. He got married at twenty one and his wife was twenty; why the rush in commitment. I understand why people get married early these days but I don't get why they were married so young.

The image was hard to decipher. It didn't seem human. I could see an oval attached to a curved line. What the hell was it? I had never seem anything like it and it didn't seem like the image had been taken by a camera.
He spoke with tears in his eyes.
"That was my little girl. Anna. Anna Jennifer Saunders."
"I never knew you had a daughter. What is that? That photo?"
"It's an ultrasound image. It was a way to monitor foetuses, made pregnancies more real because you could see it. I don't have a daughter."
"But you just said..."
"She was never born. Well, not really but I guess she was. She was stillborn. My wife miscarried when she was seven months pregnant. She hadn't felt her move in a few days and she

was worried. I should have put more credence into what she said. I took her to the doctor and she said...she said that Anna was dead. The cord," he cleared his throat "must have wrapped around her throat. She was too far gone to have an abortion so she had to give birth to her. There is nothing worse than going through all that pain to hold a cold dead child in your arms. We buried a week after she was born. She would be twenty six. Today would have been her twenty sixth birthday. I always come here on her birthday."

"I am sorry for your loss but why did you bring me here? I don't understand; this is personal for you. Why bring me here?"
"Because, Elektra you are the closest thing I have had to a daughter since Anna. The other girls that have come and gone have never been like daughters. One day, you may need to know this place. I want you to know that this a safe haven, if you ever got lost or into trouble come here. I'll be waiting, okay?"
"You think of me as a daughter? I think of you as a...a...father figure. Only one I can remember. Okay."
"I know you do. Remember this place, goose. Remember. Come here."

That's where my memory ends. He had a daughter and he lost her. He lost the most important

Darkness

thing before everything become so twisted. It
explains why his marriage disintegrated and why
he felt the way he did with me. He always wanted
children and I guess he didn't want to try again
and I was a scared child, looking for guidance
and answers. I was his daughter; he was my
father. He's raised me and never asked for
anything in return. We were always closer, we
shared a closer bond. I was an orphan and he was
a grieving father, of course we would share a
more profound bond than we shared with the
others.

He said he would be there if I got into trouble.
I guess being shot is a form of trouble. I have
to go with my instincts. He has to be there, I
mean he has to be. Losing me would have been
more painful to John. Roman would have lost a
girl he's fancied for the longest time. He'd
move on. But John. John would have lost his
daughter again. I can't believe I was selfish
enough to contemplate leaving him. Death would
have been self indulgent; I have people that
still need me.

It's a few miles away but I should be able to
make it there by dawn. I'm in agony but I have
to carry on. I have to give myself a reason and
a purpose. I can't be useless. I should be
walking around at all. The dates have changed, a
fortnight is no longer long enough. I need more

time to recover. Ow.

If I run, it will sting like a bitch but I
should be able to get there even faster. At this
rate, I could quite easily be a marathon runner.
I'm no stranger to distance running. The faster
I am, the greater the distance I put between me
and the camp. No one is stopping me. I have to
do this. I have to be the one to find him; it's
almost like he wants me to be the one as
confirmation that he hasn't lost another person.
I have to be the one to give him that piece of
mind. There is no choice in it. I owe him. I owe
him the truth. The truth behind what I did.

I must have been running for about an hour.
I need to sit and get my breath back. I need to
recover from the stitch that seems to be tearing
my lungs apart and the physical stitches that
have been inhibiting my movement. I'm so nearly
there. Just a few streets but I need to sit. I
have to find a bench or something, just five
minutes. The darkness is easing, creating a
morning mist and haze.
But this gives me time to view the stars. They
are so beautiful. The one constant in the sky.
Everything changes but they remain, unaffected.
They have been there for millions upon billions
of years. They live and they die. As one dies,
another is born. A constant cycle of birth and
death. Billions upon billions of stars. Planets

relying on them for every elements, light and
heat. Life. Death. The only constant.
The haze makes it difficult to see anything but
it's comforting to know that they are always
there. They may not be visible but they are
always there, unchanged. It's a nice feeling,
hopeful almost.

I have to force myself up. I just have a few
more meters. I can do it. Fight through the
pain. I walk down the street. There is no life
there anymore.

I finally reach the street. It's a typical
suburban street with a load of semi detached
houses, pitched against an industrial backdrop.
A perfect little piece of suburbia. The typical
houses of the working middle classes. With their
mortgages and white picket fences. What a
contrast now. Money can't buy you anything these
days. If you want something, you scavenge.
Simple as. It's not complicated. Money only
complicates things.

John's house. It's overwhelming ordinary. Semi
detached. Pebble dashed walls. It looks exactly
the same as when I was last here. Nothing has
changed in six years, that's rare. He has to be
in there, I can see an overturned rubbish bin.
It could be another camp that was scavenging
here but I'm going with my intuition and my

Darkness

intuition tells me that he's here. I can't have
just put myself through physical hell,agony, to
have it be futile. I walk up to the door. Damn,
there's a smear of blood on the door. How does
that, I mean really? I push against the door.
It's locked. Of course it would be, John lost
the key in a moment of chaos a few years. He was
devastated and after he showed me the photo, I
understood why.

I have one of two options. Neither is going to
be pleasant for me. Neither is going to pleasant
for anyone. Option one: I find the open window
we went through when we came here last. That
would involve putting pressure on my wound; bad
idea. Option two: I break the glass of the back
door and unlock it that way. I don't need to cut
myself on glass. I'm still recovering for major
internal trauma, I don't need to lose anymore
blood at the current time. Two equally terrible
ideas. Both are likely to cause me a massive
amount of pain. Both are likely to scare the
crap out of whoever is inside.

I have to use the window. If I take a run up,
maybe I tuck and roll in like a ninja. I don't
really fancy breaking John's house, he does seem
quite fond of it. Now, I just have to hope that
the window is open. It has to be; I'm sure the
lock was busted to keep it that way. I walk
around to the side of the house, listening to

any sounds that may indicate life inside the house. The window seems like it is open, just a crack. Result. I just have to put a little bit of pressure on the window, open it just enough to get my entire body. I've grown considerably since I last went through this window. I'm slim, but I am a lot more muscular than I was at the age of thirteen.

I think I have enough of a gap. Right, I just have to get a run up and jump. Whether this works or not, I have no clue. If it does, great but if it doesn't I will go head first into the window, knocking myself out. I'll give myself a fifty meter run up, that should do it. Okay, here goes nothing. On the count of three. One...two...three.

Ow! Ow!
I'm through but Jesus Christ! That is bound to have done some damage. Shit, shit shit! Ow! At least I'm through; John, you'd better be here you bastard. It's a good thing Rita's taken my stitches out otherwise I would be in trouble. That would be finish me off well and truly. My abdomen hasn't half been through a beating the past month. Before, I'd had a few minor scars but now my stomach looks horrific. Damn it, this is going to sting for a good few weeks or months yet.

Darkness

I stand.
The force puts pressure on my lungs, forcing me
to cough. I begin to have a coughing fit. A
violent coughing fit. My lungs feel like they
are on fire. All of my coughing ends with a
handful of blood. Oh my god. I think I'm in
trouble.
I look up.
Looking up at a bedraggled, wild eyed man.
John.

Darkness

Chapter 14

"John?"
"Elektra?"
I run to him but he rebuffs me. What is up with him? He looks dishevelled and unshaven. I've never seen him like this. His eyes are blood shot and he stinks. With the greatest of respect, he smells stale, like off whiskey or gin. He must have been drinking. Bloody idiot. Why would he rebuke me? Did he not want to be found and if not, why? Does he not feel any form of duty to us?

What has he done to himself?

Darkness

"Have you been here the entire time? What the bloody hell were you playing at? You've scared all of us sick! How could you do that to us, you selfish bastard?"
He just squints at me, as if trying to decipher what I'm saying. He's never looked at me like that before, as if he doesn't know me or recognise me. What the hell has happened?

"Piss off, you're dead. I shall stay here and stew, now piss off." He steps toward me and slaps me. He slapped me. It takes me a few seconds to recover from that. I can taste a weird metallic substance in my mouth. Blood. I knew he was a powerful bastard but I didn't think I would ever experience his fist in my face. Wait, he thinks I'm dead? Why does he think I'm dead? Why would he believe that a bullet would be the thing that finally killed me off.

"John, it's me. I'm not dead. See." I place my finger inside my mouth and show him the blood from my split lip. Yeah, that proves I'm alive doesn't it? Only living things bleed; if it bleeds you can kill it. Please let this be the proof.
He takes my hand and just stares at it intensely. He looks from my hand to my face, my hand to my face. He looks like he's in shock. Like I'm some kind of supernatural being. Also,

he knows he's in trouble because he just slapped me; it didn't end too well for the last person that did that.

"John, it's me. It's really me. Look at me."
"Elektra? How..."
"I survived. The bullet did some damage but not enough to kill me. Enough to put me out of commission but not to kill me."
"My girl, I am so sorry."
He scoops me into his arms and embraces me. It's a lovely reunion but all I can think about is this mouth full of blood that I need to spit. The taste of blood, not pleasant. He squeezes me and my mouth full of bloody saliva releases itself onto his back. I don't think he's noticed. He can find another shirt. Eek.

He looks at me again. His grey eyes swimming with tears; I don't need this bullshit reunion at this time. I know I've wanted this reality to be true for the longest time but I am in too much pain. The slap to the face didn't help matters. Now, not only does my abdomen kill me, my mouth aches as well. Wonderful; at least I didn't lose any teeth. I'm not attractive enough to pull off the no front teeth appearance.

"Are you okay? I'm sorry but...you're the third Elektra I've seen today. Admittedly, you're the only one that spoke. The rest were

Darkness

just...corpses."
"Sh...it's okay. I'm here, you probably saw
three of me because you are pissed out off your
tree. Don't deny it. Did you really think a
piece of metal could kill me? Don't be
delusional. Answer my question, have you been
here the whole time?"
"Yes. I told you to come here, if you got into
trouble and you did. You didn't tell the others
did you? I can't deal with seeing the rest of
them."
"No, I didn't tell them anything. I remembered.
This place has not changed at all, has it? You
could have left the front door unlocked so I
didn't have to knock the wind out of my sails."
"Well when you go back, don't tell them where I
am. I can't leave the door open, anyone could
get in."
"Wait, when I get back? Don't you mean we? I'm
not going with out you; I've stuck my neck on
the line for this."
"Elektra, don't make this difficult. I'm not
going back or I would have already, goose. I'm
not going back."

What does he mean he's not going back? How can
he even say that? Everyone back at the camp
misses him, needs him even. I can't believe he
could even contemplate. I know one thing: I'm
not leaving without him, no matter whether I
have his permission or not.

Darkness

"Goose, I can't go back there...."
"Stop being obdurate..."
"No, I can't," he interrupts.
"Why?"
"Because I'm dying! Are you happy now Elektra?
I'm dying."

What? How? How can he...he be...dying? I have
spent hours thinking that I would be the one to
find him, dead. I just had vision. If there is a
cloud deity, he's a bastard with a great love of
irony or something like that. He gives me hope
for a matter of minutes to rip it away from me.
That's why he doesn't want to go back. He wants
to die here for what it's worth. I cannot
believe this is happening. I was supposed to be
the one that was dying; not John, who was always
the pillar and authoritarian of the camp. This
can't be real.

"How do you know, you silly git? I mean you
can't have proof or anything."
"It's what I've been thinking for a long time.
My memory went to shit and I couldn't coordinate
anything properly. Rita told me she thought I
had a condition called sporadic CJD, one of the
symptoms is like a fast acting dementia. Loss of
intellect. Hallucinations. I don't want to lose
my mind; I don't want to be helpless, stewing in
my own juices and trapped in my body like some

kind of vegetable. So I made my choice; I'm
going to overdose. Greatest chance of death,
less mess."
"No...no," I can barely get the words out
"I have the pills. I just need someone to help
me with the cap; I can't open lids anymore."

"You could make a cup of coffee two weeks
ago..."
"A lot can change in two weeks, goose. I just
need you to do this for me. I either do this now
or the others will find me and I will die in
that cramped bloody house. A vegetable. Do you
want that for me? Hm? Please do this for me."
"No. What are you asking me to do? What are you
asking for? Euthanasia? No; bullshit. Rita might
be wrong."
"No, she's not. I have to have it; I don't
recognise half of the people in that camp. I
don't even remember what Isla looked like. I
haven't for years goose. Yes, I'm asking you to
give me a mercy killing. I want to die Elektra,
please do this for me. I have never asked
anything from you!"
"That's true but how can you ask this of me? I
will have to leave with that. Killing you. How
can I live with that you egocentric sod? If you
want to top yourself, do it yourself. I am done
having to kill people."

How can he ask me to kill him? He has been like

Darkness

a father to me so how can he ask me to end his
life? If he does have this condition, then it
may be the kindest thing but we should discuss
our plan of action as a group. This can't be my
choice alone. He's pleading with me. Why do
people keep pleading with me to do things that
are too much of me? This isn't fair but then
again, life isn't fair. Why did I think
everything was going to be okay? Am I really
that naïve?

"Elektra, what do you by 'people'? What
happened? How did you get shot?"
"You want to know the truth. I left Roman; I got
jumped; he shot me and I slit his throat. I
killed him and you want to know the worst thing,
I don't care anymore. I killed a man who was
trying to provide for the people he cared about;
he could have had a wife or children and I
murdered him in cold blood. I can't be a
murderer anymore so if you want to arrange your
execution, that's on you. Please don't do this
to me, I need you. We all do."
Now I'm pleading with him, how the tides turn.

"You did what you had to do. To survive. You
have so much more to give; you're young. You're
going to do amazing things with your life, I
know you will. Kid, you deserve all the
happiness in the world and I'm sorry I won't be
there to see it. But please, I'm old and I'm

tired of fighting and losing. Please help me. I
am in pain, Elektra. I just want to be free.
Freedom. I love you baby girl. You're going to
be fine without me, I know it."

I can't do it. I don't deserve happiness. I
deserve to be tortured; I deserve everything
that's happening now. I'm not going to be fine.
I need him. It will be like losing my family all
over again and I can't deal with that. I don't
want to lose him but is it really my choice?
He's stubborn. There's no convincing him
otherwise. Whether he has my blessing or not,
today his life ends. I can't believe I'm saying
this. I can't be. I don't want him to be in
pain. I have to set him free. This is the one
thing he asks; how can I refuse? I mean, wasn't
this decision I was going to make? I was going
to die. I am so many things but a hypocrite
isn't one of them. If he suffers, it's all on
me. I can't live with that but I can't live with
helping him die. This is the one and only he's
asking of me; the only thing I could never do.
The only thing I can't refuse to do. I have to
help. I'm going to hell anyway, oh wait I'm
already there.

"What bottle do you need?"
"What?"
"What bottle are you going to down?"
"The paracetamol with the Jack Daniels."

Darkness

"Good choice; I'll go and get them. Is there anything else you need?"
"No. Elektra?"
"What?"
"Thank you," he whispers with a smile on his lips.

I have to keep myself together. Neither of us need the bullshit. This is the most painful thing I've ever had to do. Not only am I losing a father, but I'm losing a mentor and a confidant. I'm losing my best friend. Oh god, I'm falling to pieces. He's going to die; he's going to die. Oh god. Oh god! I have to do this for him but god, why? Why, you sadistic arsehole? Why do you see fit to take away everyone I have ever loved or cared about? Anyone I can't kill; the only one I could never kill.

I place the pills on the table and unscrew the lid. I then go over the mini bar in the corner of the room and pick up a bottle of Jack Daniels. I unscrew the lid from that bottle and place two glasses in front of us. If I'm going to do this, I don't want to remember it. I pour the dark, sour liquor into both cups. He looks at me and smiles.

He's shaking. He pours the contents of the bottle, three or four pills, into his mouth and

Darkness

downs the glass of whiskey. He gags but forces
them down. He sighs contentedly. I take the
bottle and drink. It takes vile but I need to be
numb. Drunk. Ignorant.

"Elektra, thank you."
"You've already thanked me. Don't make this
anymore difficult."
"No, thank you for being in my life. You were
the daughter I always wanted. Tell Rita to look
after herself and tell Erin that I'm sorry.
Also, give that Roman kid a chance; he's a good
man. You deserve each other."
"I already have." I have to blink back the tears
"That's my girl. I owe you the truth. Your
parents, I knew them. I stole you from them.
Elektra, forgive me. I think they're still
alive"
"I don't care, it's okay. Just get comfortable."

Wait, did he just my parents are alive? Why
would he steal me? I don't want to think about
it. He is about to die; I can't bring myself to
think so badly of him. I don't want that memory
of him in my head. I want to remember him
younger and strong. I want to remember him
taking me on hunts, just talking to me. I want
to remember the man who was the most important
person in my life. That's the John I want to
remember. Not this broken shell of a man in
front of me.

Darkness

"Have a good life, goose. You've earned it;
don't let anyone tell you that you aren't good
enough or strong enough because you are. You are
beautiful and smart and so, so brave."
"Shut up you cheesy old git, you."
"That's my girl."

His eyes roll back into his head. His breathing
becomes laboured. Then...silence. Nothing. I
walk over to him and take his pulse.
He's gone. He's dead.

Oh my god, he's actually dead. I helped him. How
could I help him? The dawn finally breaks. John
always used to say it's always darkest before
the dawn, I never knew he's die by it. John
Marcus Saunders. Time of death: 0642. Oh my god,
he's gone. For good. I've lost him. It's my
fault. He was looking for an excuse to get away.
I can't leave him here. I have to take him back
to the others. They have to know. But they can't
know about this place. His true home. I'm not
going to take that away from him, even in death.

I can't leave him like this. He looks like a
broken alcoholic. I have to do something. The
last thing I can do. The beard. It's the beard
that makes him look like that. I pick up the
pill bottle. I walk into the bathroom again. I
place the bottle back down in the medicine

cabinet. Amazing what is kept in a medicine cabinet. Paracetamol. Ibuprofen. Ribbed condoms, maybe the most disturbing. Am I really trying to be funny? That's new.

I spot a razor. Right at the back of the cabinet. If I can get some water, I can do this. He has to be presentable; the corpse in the arm chair is not John. It's but a shadow of him. If the beard were to go, he would look exactly as he did when he left. I owe him that. I owe him everything. I walk into the kitchen and turn on the hot tap. I place a scourer in the lukewarm water. I then walk over to John. I heard that using hot water water opens up the pores, do you think it still does? He won't feel it but I feel I owe him the respect of treating him as if he will. How can I do this? Why did I let myself be persuaded? He knew all the right thing to say to convince me. How do I even know that was Rita's diagnosis? Bastard could have lied to me. No. I can't think of him that badly. He's dead. He's dead because of me. Because of me.

I wipe his face with the sponge side of the scourer. Most of the dirt that lay on his skin has been removed. I have to detach myself. If I succumb to emotion, I won't be able to continue. Game over. This is what he wanted. He wouldn't want anyone to be upset by his death. This isn't death, this is his liberation. He will not have to continue suffering. He's finally free.

I walk over to the cold tap. It takes a while
for the water to flow but when it does, there is
a lot of mud and bits of vegetation in it. I
place the razor underneath the cold water tap;
blood seems to come straight off of the razor's
edge. I'm not surprised it was used a weapon. I
must have been.

I saunter back over to John. How can he look
like he's sleeping? How is that possible? The
first pleasant death I've seen: no one coughing
up their guts, begging for oxygen and no blood
covered corpse. He's found peace. I begin to
shave his neck, being careful not to nip his
neck with the blade. I just have to be careful.
I've never shaved a man before. I never thought
the first man I'd shave would be a dead body.
I've shaved before so I have an idea of what to
do. He's just a dead body. John is gone. He's
gone. There is no life in him.

I'm done. There was minimal damage to him. A few
cuts but nothing significant. That's the John I
remember. A little stubble, no more. He looks so
peaceful. I hope he finds peace, wherever he is.
God knows, he deserves it. He's done more than
his fair share.

How do I get him back? I can't carry him. It'll

be difficult to get back on my own but with extra weight, no. I owe it to him to take him back to the camp. We burn him. Then I returns and spread his ashes here. On my own. My own. I'm the only one he wanted to know about this place. I have to find a mode of transport.

I open the back door and look back. How can he still look like he's sleeping? I can't think like that because I will try to bring him back. I could do it. If I were to make him vomit, he might stand a chance but he would hate me for the rest of his days. I can't do that to him. I have to let him go. I get a way out of here and then I take him back with me to the camp.

As soon as I step outside, I'm greeted by putrid breath and a set of yellowing teeth. It's a horse. The beginning of John's animal farm but I'm grateful. I have a way to get us both out of here. I just have to get him onto the horse. I just have to overcome that small difficulty. I drag him by his feet. I never thought I'd be this but there is no dignity I could give him. He is...was... a big lump. Not fat but muscular. Now, I just have to muster my strength and chuck him on the back of the horse. I'm strong. I've lifted people a long way before. Not with a chunk out of me but I can do this. I have to do this. For him.

140

Darkness

Right. He's on. My back went but he's on the
horse. I'll have to ride carefully. If he fell
off, I won't be able to put him back on the
horse. No dignity for him. Failure for me. Once
I get back to the flat, then I can deal with
what I'm feeling but now I have to conceal it. I
owe him that. Why do I owe him so much? I owe
him things I can never repay if I live for
decades.

The horse is tame. John had already saddled it.
What was he planning to do? I've never ridden a
horse before. I wanted to avoid it but this is
my ticket out of here. It's my one way ticket to
Wales or Scotland. My liberation. Why did John's
liberation have to be in death? Liberty in
death, the only true freedom. I hoist myself
onto the horse. I ache. I always ache. I
shouldn't complain. I'm lucky if anything.

I keep one hand behind my back, keeping him in
place. He feels so cold. All of the nights when
we were out hunting, I relied on his warmth. He
always seemed like a heater, never cold. He
radiated warmth, both literally and
metaphorically. How can he really be gone? How
can he be gone? How am I supposed to cope
without him?Pull yourself together, Elektra.

I manage to get the horse into a trot. This was
probably the worst way to travel under the

Darkness

circumstances. I have to keep on. Fight through
the pain, that's what he always said. Fight
through the pain. The sunlight invades every
part of the landscape. Sunlight; the light at
the end of the tunnel. If only that were true
and not a load of pretentious bullshit.

I have to bring him home.

Darkness

Chapter 15

I have been riding for about half an hour and
that's when I see the first person. Annie. It's
good to see her up and about. She looks pale and
sickly but alive. My handiwork turned out pretty
good. She's using crutches but at least she can
use her legs. Oh damn, they've sent out a damn
search party out after me. I'm in trouble. Deep
trouble.

"Elektra! Where have you been? Rita and Roman
have been looking all night, since you left.
Where did you go? Who's that on the back of the
horse? Can I have the horse?"
"I've had some things to take care off; none of

your business nosy. It doesn't matter, don't look at it Annie. Yeah, I got the horse for all of us so we have to take care of it, okay?"
"Oh okay, yay! Shall I go back and tell the others that you're back? I think you're going to be in trouble though; Rita didn't look happy."
"No. No. I'm heading back anyway. I know I am. Tell the other kids on patrol to come back to the camp. I have to say something important, okay? Don't question it, just do it."
"Okay. See you later Elektra."

Of course I'm in trouble. I ran away. I did what John did. I knew the implications of my choice and what my disobedience would bring but I still went. I'm glad I did or I may have missed the last chance to say goodbye to the best man I've ever known. I regret nothing. I ride a little further until I'm right outside. I take a deep breath. I have to go into this as serenely as possible.

I dismount the horse and open the front door. Shit's about to go down, I can feel it in my waters. The first sight to greet me is Roman. He's holding a plate or something and he just instinctively drops it. We just stand staring at each other, like in a Western stand off. Last Chance Saloon and all that stuff. He runs to me and embraces me. He's not mad? I escaped from his grip, scared him and he has nothing to say.

144

Darkness

Why isn't he saying anything? Why isn't he
screaming at me? I just want someone to blame
me. I deserve to be blamed.

"Don't ever do that again, you bitch. I have
never been so worried about you as I have been
the past month. I need you, don't leave me
again."
"Roman, he's...dead. John...he's...dead."

He draws away from me. My emotions are deceiving
me yet again because I can feel tears on my
cheeks again. He looks as shocked as I've ever
seen him. I shouldn't have sprung it on him so
early but I could lie to him and convince him
everything was alright when it's not.
"How do you know?" He wipes the tears off of my
cheeks.
"That's where I went. I found him and
he...he...was dying. So I did what he asked of
me. He begged me Roman. I...I...helped him."
"Oh my god. We have to tell the others. How did
you help him? I won't judge you Lex. I'm sure
you did what you had to."
"He needed help opening pill bottles. I
unscrewed the lid. I might have well as shoved
the pills down his throat. What are we going to
do?"
"John was a good man. If he asked you to do
something, you did it. Don't feel sorry honey.
Come here, it's going to be alright."

Darkness

I step back.
"How the hell is everything going to be alright?
He's dead, Roman! Dead! He's not coming back,
end of! How can you say that?"
I let out a scream at the top of my lungs. I've
needed release. How am I supposed to keep
control when people spout off such bullshit.
It's an insult to think everything's going to be
fine; he's called me callous in the past. The
only problem with the volume of my voice: I'm
met with four pairs of confused eyes. Shit,
shit, shittity, shit, shit.

This isn't how they should have found out. I
must looked half crazed. I've never shouted like
that before in front of them but do I care? Yes.
I do. Damn. Most of them have run off but one
stays, just glaring at me. David. He's twelve.
Twelve with the mind of a forty year old. He's
shown promise as a doctor or a scientist. Rita's
taught him how to produce morphine and basic
antibiotics that are easy to produce naturally.
We're all orphans here but he lost his parents
when he was a year old. If what John said is
true, then I'm not. My parents may still be out
there, wondering what happened to the daughter.
That doesn't matter anyway. John was the only
father I've ever had and will ever have. As far
as I'm concerned, my dad is dead. My biological
father is just blood; it takes more than blood

to be a father.

"Calm down Lex. First thing, where is he?"
I take a few deep breaths to keep myself from
hyperventilating.
"Lex?"
"He's on the horse. Outside. I couldn't leave
him there...I couldn't."
"You have a horse? How'd you swing that one?
Anyway, we bring him in and then we...we go from
there, okay? There's no need for a breakdown."
"You said everything's going to be fine when
it's not. It's not. It can't be. That's the
truth of it all. Lie to me all you want but
don't lie to yourself Roman."

I brush past him and walk up the stairs. I can't
deal with this. I thought I could be strong and
keep my emotions at bay but no. I'm not strong
enough to deal with this. I've never been strong
enough to deal with this. I can only see one
positive, well two. John is at peace and if I
can let John go, I can kill anyone if I have to.
I can say that with confidence. Roman will go
outside and bring him in. I just want to sleep.
I've done my part. I just want to be on my own
right now. I was there when he died, that is on
me. I'm the only one who knows what it was like
to watch John die. Only me. I think I've earned
the right to wallow.

Darkness

I collapse down on the bed. I want to feel numb. That's all I want but I can't. I drank that vile liquid to be lost in an alcoholic haze but nothing. Nothing. This day has been the worst of my life. How can I cope with this? How can he expect that of me? He can't. He can't. Why would he do that to me? The bastard. Why did the only thing he asked of me have to be the toughest thing I've ever down? I can't even feel this way about the man I murdered but I do about just opening a bottle. I can't be detached. I want to be. I don't want to feel loss or pain but I guess I don't have a choice. Nobody gets the break from that. No one can be that detached. That's life. Bastarding life.

I am exhausted.
I am in pain.
I just want a release. I want sleep.

I hear the door open. Then a few minutes later, it closes. I feel sick. I hadn't realised how sick until now. I rush to the bin and release the contents of my stomach. I can't control it. Like I can't control the tears coming out of my eyes. My insides are burning, just like my outsides. Bile and out of date whiskey. That's all there is in my stomach. I just want an end to all this. I have no dignity left. I could die like this. Folded over a cheap, decrepit paper bin. The inside of my nostrils and throat burn

Darkness

like someone has shoved a flaming torch down my
windpipe.
I am sick. I am tired. I just need to go to
sleep. I just need to forget.

I had hoarded Valerian at one point. I have my
own supplies. Sometimes my kleptomania is a good
thing. I chew the root, begging for relief. I am
a hundred percent done. I done with all the
bullshit. This is never getting better. Just
when it looks like it is, some other shit or
piss comes raining down.

I can feel myself getting more and more light
headed but I can't let go. I hear the door open.
Oh my god, why does he not get the hint? If I
wanted human company, I wouldn't have come up
here. I desire to be left alone. Why does no one
understand that? I hate it.

"Elektra, can I talk to you?"
"No. Piss off."
He walks in anyway and sits on the ground next
to me. He begins to rub my back. If he doesn't
get his hands off of me, I will break his hand.
It's been that kind of day; it wouldn't be
hardship. I feel more bile rising in the back of
my throat. I'm about to bring up the Valerian.
Damn it. I regurgitate the contents of my
stomach again.
"It's okay, bring it all up. Sh...that's it.

149

Darkness

Come on, get it all up."

I can't stop vomiting. I don't know why. There
is nothing for me to throw up and yet it keeps
coming up. I don't want Roman here. I want to be
left alone to wallow in self pity. I don't need
a bloody audience.
"I'll get Rita, see if she can get you anything
for the sickness. Don't move."
Where the hell am I going to go? Mars?
What a stupid bloody thing to say.
But at least I'm alone again. I can hear a the
girls next door sobbing; I would say it's
pitiful but they have a right to grieve. We all
do. I do need something. The Valerian must have
irritated my stomach. If I felt like death
before, now I feel like death on a crap day.

I can hear footsteps. It's probably Roman again.
If I take the bin back to the bed with me, I may
be able to sleep or something. Sleep deprived
and chucking up. Damn. Damn. Damn.

"I have peppermint, ginger and spearmint. It's
all she has. They should ease the vomiting.
Here."
I gaze up at him and, cautiously, accept the
herbs. I chew the spearmint, I cannot stand
peppermint. The smell of the spearmint is almost
refreshing. Still making me gag but I'm willing
to do anything to make the regurgitation cease.

Darkness

I feel slightly better. I'm trying to hold down
the mint. That and the whiskey would be a gag
worthy concoction. This is taking my mind off of
things but my injury feels like fire. It feels
like it's burning me. Ah.

I walk over to the bed. I place the bin by the
side of the bed and I lay on my side. It's the
only way I can get somewhat comfortable, if
that's even possible. Roman comes and sit next
to on the bed. He continues to rub my back as if
he is winding a baby. It's really not helping.

"We're thinking about how we deal with John.
Whether we bury him and cremate him. When you're
ready."
I don't need to think about that now.
"We cremate him, Roman. It's what we always do.
Why should it be any different?"
"Are you sure you're okay with that? I mean-"
"Yes, I'm sure."
"Okay. If you're sure Lex."

I want to be alone but I also want him here. I
want comfort. I need comfort or reassurance. I
want blame but I want reassurance.
I let my eyes close. If I will for sleep, maybe
it will work. Roman sits, staring at me while
stroking my back. John was right; he's a good
man. Decent. I don't deserve him at all. He
begins to trace the line of my spine, drawing

patterns across my back. I feel safe with Roman. I can let myself fall asleep, I think.

He doesn't take his eyes off of me. The last time he did, I escaped. I ran to a dying man. He's not going to let that happen again, I can tell. I have to let myself go. I'm too tired to cry. Shittest day of my life so far.

"Just go to sleep Lex. It'll look better in the morning. Somehow. You've been through a trauma. You've been traumatised too many times in the past few weeks. I will never let anything bad happen to you again, Lex. I swear to you. I'm going to protect you, if I can. Will you let me? Will you let me protect you Lex?"

He thinks he can protect me. How naïve is he? There is nothing in this world that can keep any of us safe. He thinks there is a choice to safety and protection, as if by muttering an answer I'll be exempt from all harm.
But the offer does make me think. He wants to be there for me. Why? Why does he want to protect me? Why does he even fancy me in the first place? I'm a stubborn, spiteful, vindictive venomous bitch with no control over my emotions. I can't chose not to feel because the day I do is the day I lose the right to call myself human.
I don't deserve the offer of companionship. I

Darkness

don't deserve companionship full stop. The thing
is I can't stop thinking about my answer.

"Yes," I mutter.
"Good, I love you Lex."

Chapter 16

When I wake up, it's dawn again. I must have been asleep for a day at least. My head feels fuzzy. I raise my hand to my forehead, trying to get relief from the fire in my head. Migraine. The pain is a distraction. I begin to think about going to find John again when it falls on me like a tonne of bricks. John is dead. I helped to kill him. It wasn't a nightmare.

I can't move. Everything is spinning. The light burns. Yeah, definitely a migraine. I have to squint to see anything. Roman is sitting in the corner of the room with a mug of tea in his hands. He takes a sip. He stares at the ceiling as if there is something intriguing up there. He

154

hasn't noticed I'm awake yet. How long has he been sitting there? I didn't think he'd leave. Of course he wouldn't. I am secretly quite glad. He hasn't abandoned me.

But he said he loved me. How can he love me? He doesn't even know me. He may think he does but he has no idea about the real me; behind the cold, bitter exterior. He knows what he wants to know and makes up the rest about me like the way he thinks I need to be protected. I have been ready to leave the country for years, on my own. I can protect myself. Emotions and sentiment make me weak as I've learnt. Caring is not an advantage. Love is not an advantage.

He suddenly notices me.
"Wakey wakey sleepy head. I thought you were in a coma; thanks for the reassurance."
"How long have I been out?" I state groggily.
"Three days, I think. Yeah, three days. I've never seen someone sleep for three days that wasn't in some kind of medically induced coma, hence the assumption. Do you remember what's going on?"
"Three days? Shit. Yes, I do. John's dead; have you dealt with him already? Cremated him?"
"No," he pauses "We were waiting until you woke up. Everyone should be there; we all have a right to say goodbye to him Lex. Deal with him? Funny choice of words. Almost sounds like you

don't care about what happens which would be complete rubbish wouldn't it my dear? You're not exactly discreet when it comes to your feelings towards John."

No I'm not am I Roman? But I have to conceal the way I feel about him because I won;t be able to cope with this. I don;t need this patronising sympathetic crap. How is it possible for someone to be so blatantly wrong about something? I am not going to say anything; his question isn't worthy of a response. He's trying to play the hero as if I'm a damsel in distress. It is complete and utter bullshit.

He is such a vacuous moron. Spouting off false emotions and then promising to protect me against death, give me a break. I was over emotional when I said yes. What was I thinking? I've given him permission to play the hero. He would have taken any excuse and now, he's using my vulnerability against me. Oh god, he's good. He would have done anything to have an excuse to use my emotions as a way to seduce me. Yes, he doesn't love me. He just wants to get into my knickers and any excuse would have done. Death or illness. Oh he's a manipulative bastard. That's all they want to do; manipulate me to have their way with me. You see why I wanted to be as far away from humanity ass possible.

Darkness

"You shouldn't have wasted the time. He's going to start going off. I've already said goodbye so you'll excuse me if I won't be standing watching him burn. Go on, tell Rita to get the bonfire ready. It's time to cook him."
"Do you have to put it so graphically? I understand if you don't want to watch the cremation, that's fine, but why be so angst about it? It'll be happening later today, if you change your mind, okay? Would you like some tea or coffee to tide you over?"

It's going to be drugged. I know it. Any bloody excuse. He must have injected me with something when I was vomiting so I would be distracted and wouldn't notice it. I mean I am desensitised to needles. It's the only explanation. I don't trust him. I feel like I'm burning up. They've drugged me already; they're all in on it.

"Don't worry, I won't no. No. If I want anything, I'll get it myself. I just want to be alone, I think I have a migraine coming on. I have my own supplies to deal with it. Go on then. Go off and talk to people."
"God, you're irritable. I'm going, I'm going. You know I love it when you get all moody on me."
I bet you do you incongruous bastard. He walks over to and kisses my head. I don't have the strength to pull away so I let him.

Darkness

"I love you. Treating me like shit will do
nothing to deter me, you know. It hasn't
deterred me before. Think about it."

He doesn't get it. I know. I don't know what I
know but I do. I think. I don't know, my head is
so blurred and now it's getting intense.
Everything is so blurred and jumbled. I don't
feel in control of my own head. My own body.
I've been drugged. I must have been. Have I
already said that? Damn.
I still feel like I'm burning up. I'm sweating
but it's freezing in this room. It always is.
How am I sweating? I haven't done anything
strenuous. I slide so I'm sitting with my feet
hanging over the side of the bed. Ow, my head. I
need to open a window. I need air. I'm being
suffocated. There's no air in here. I just have
to get to the window.

My legs are still and uncoordinated. There is
not a single part of me that doesn't burn or
ache or sting. Everything is spinning. I can't
gain my balance. I just need to balance. My
entire body is weak. I just have to hope for the
best. I take one step and nearly fall, only
saving myself by holding onto the bed. I just
have to keep putting one foot in front of the
other. This isn't real. Nothing is spinning.
That's just my mind and eyes working together to
deceive me.

Darkness

I make it to the window. The window needs a good
tug before it opens but when it does, it is the
first bit of relief I've felt. It's no cooling
me down but I finally have good oxygen in my
lungs. Air. I don't feel so suffocated. The only
problem is I still feel dizzy. I feel faint.

If I just stay here and get my air into my
lungs, I should be okay. I should be. Whether I
will be is another matter entirely. I have to
get back to the flat, make plans fast. Then, I
can think all of this through but there is one
thing I know for certain: I am not going to the
cremation but I'm not leaving him with them. I
will take his ashes and spread them over his
home. Allow him to stay there as he desired. I
can't let them know; they'll try and stop me.
They can't stop me. God, don't let them stop me.
Am I really asking him for help? He's the most
manipulative of them all. The original
puppeteer.

I can't get enough air. I'm being suffocated
again. What have they done to me? What is
happening to me? Am I dying? Again? Breathe
in....and out. In and out. Focus on that. If I
focus on my breathing then maybe it will make it
better. Oh god. I can't focus on it. How many
seconds are there supposed to be between
breaths? How many times am I supposed to blink a

minute? Everything is so blurred and painful. I can't. I can't keep myself conscious. I think my brain is being deprived of oxygen.

I can't hold on. So, I let go.

When I wake up, I feel so much worse. I must have fallen backwards. I move my hand to feel the back of my head and it feels wet. I'm bleeding. Great, I've got a migraine and now, a concussion. I'm on a bed. How did I get from the floor to a bed? Did I faint walk? Faint walking: like sleep walking only, it's when you're unconscious.

Wait. I don't recognise this room. Have I been here before? Oh my god, I've been abducted. No. I do recognise this room. I've only been in here once. This is Roman's room. He would be the one to find me, wouldn't he? Why did he lay me down on my back when I've cut the back of my head open? Is he a total ignoramus? You don't need a brain cell to know you do not place a person with a cut on the back of their head on their back.

The room smells strange. It's like a mixture of peppermint and soap. Well I say soap, more like soapy disinfectant. I like the smell but then again, I like weird smells. I love the aroma of petrol and TCP and petrichor. I even like the smell of damp. How peculiar is that? Of course I would like the smell of this room. It's also the same smell as Roman's musk. There's something almost comforting about the smell of cleanliness and the refreshing notes of the mint. There's probably rohyponol in the air; I don't know how you would do that but I'm sure they have figured it out.

I am too disorientated to get up but I am thinking I have to. I have to get going before he returns. I may have time if they are down at the cremation. I need to escape. Maybe he's not doing anything. Maybe I'm hallucinating or being paranoid. Yeah, I could be being paranoid. I hope I'm being paranoid. No. No. Ah! I can't figure things out properly anymore. I need time. Time. Do I have time?

"Elektra, you bounce back fast. You fell and hit your head. I stitched you as much as I could. Don't worry, I sterilised the needle. Do you remember anything?"

Try to stitch me up again and I will sterilise you, you patronising dimwit. Why didn't he get Rita to stitch me up? How does he know how to stitch anyone up? Does he want to kill me? God, Elektra you're already paranoid, there's no need to fill your head with thoughts of being murdered with a needle.

Darkness

"I remember. I felt faint and I fainted; no need
to look into. No need to analyse it."
He places the back of his hand against my head.
He wipes another bead of sweat from my head. I'm
still sweating like a pig. Why?

"Are you sure you're alright Lex? You're burning
up. I'll get a thermometer. Don't go anywhere."
I could muster a sarcastic response to that but
it gets boring after a time. I can't be bothered
to respond. I'm not going anywhere so I can say
thank you to captain obvious for that
revelation. That is my comment on the matter.

I hear him rustling things around in the
medicine cabinet in the bathroom next door. We
have quite a few thermometers but most of them
are with Rita. Why is he rummaging in there? Is
he looking for something else? A razor to cut
me? A piece of dental floss to squeeze the life
out of me? Maybe. If he wanted to strangle me,
he could just do it with his bare hands. He
doesn't need help.

Calm down Elektra, don't over analyse things.
You're already paranoid. Paranoia. First sign of
schizophrenia. Am I becoming schizophrenic?
Neurotic? That's all I need. Mentally ill on top
of everything else. Aren't I just the best
advocacy for the female population? I wouldn't

Darkness

take me as an example at all.

He walks through the door swiftly. I'm not going
to struggle. I'm going to do everything he says.
If he tries to kill me, I head-butt him and get
the hell out of dodge. Yes, sounds like a plan.
I have a plan. Well, I say a plan...it is
adaptable. It's a terrible plan. Then again,
I've had worse plans. Like going into a burning
old supermarket with no weapons. Yes, that
worked out so well for me last time, did it not?

"Open your mouth. Now, this thermometer may look
like it is a breeding ground for some form of
new bacteria but I have sterilised it to the
best of my ability, with TCP. So the taste may
make you gag but at least we can see if you're
running a fever."

I can smell the disinfectant without his
declaration; I have to put that thing in my
mouth. That sounded a lot dirtier than intended.
I meant a thermometer, don't judge me. I open my
mouth. I don't want to close my mouth so I let
him hold it in place. I cannot keep it in my
mouth. Can you be poisoned by TCP? I shouldn't
be worried about that. I'm more likely to get
infected by the little bit of scum at the end of
it. Oh my god, that's solidified phlegm. Oh god.
Oh god. Oh god. You nasty.
He finally removes the thermometer, about time

163

Darkness

but I'm not complaining.

"Oh god, Lex; you're burning up. You're running a fever of 41 degrees Celsius. That's what is it...Hyperpyrexia. I have to do something to get the fever down. How long have you had this fever? It's important you remember Lex. How long?"
"Since I got back."

In truth, I can't remember. It must have been since then. The migraine could explain the nausea but maybe it was the beginning of some flu or something. Maybe I'm not being drugged. It's still a possibility but I am burning up.

I need help. I'm sweating. I can feel beads of sweat running down my face like Niagara Falls. I may have to just break the fever. Sweat it out. He picks up the flannel he brought in with him and dabs my forehead. Is it possible to break this type of fever? I've heard of this before. It's usually caused by sun exposure or septicaemia. I pull my shirt up enough to see my scar. It's red raw. The skin around it is taut and red. It looks like there is some form of bruising around it. There are a few blisters around the site. One of them appears to have burst. How long have I had that?

"Oh god. Let me take your pulse. It's alright.

You might be tachycari...tachycarn..."
"Tachycardic."
"Yeah. I never claimed to be a doctor unlike
you, smart arse."

He puts his hand against my neck just by my
trachea. He pulls away after six seconds.
"140 beats a minute. I have to get you to Rita.
Damn the cremation, this is more important. Lift
your arms and legs up."
"No," I mutter "he deserves the respect of a
cremation. I can wait. Call her when it's
finished; you should be down there with them."
"No. I've said my goodbyes. Your life and
keeping you alive is more important to me than
saying goodbye. I'm not going to say goodbye to
a cadaver over trying to save you Lex."

Why is he so desperate to play the knight in
shining armour? All of my symptoms make sense. I
wanted to believe I'd been drugged but no. All
of the signs point to septicaemia. Sepsis of the
blood. I've got a bacterial infection flowing
through my blood. How long have I had it? Has
the bacteria been in my blood since the bullet?
Has it been festering in my blood for over two
weeks? If I can't get antibiotics or magic
bullets, I'm dead. I will go into septic shock
where my blood pressure will drop to a dangerous
level, leading to not enough oxygenated blood
reaching my organs. Multiple organ failure.

Darkness

Death. What stage of sepsis am I at? I'm dying at this moment but why has it taken so long to manifest itself? Did I get it from John's window? I did cut myself but how? How?

Am I going to die? After everything? Is this my punishment for aiding John to his death? For my callous existence? I did face the odds just to die because of something that is a glorified lodger. He needs to say goodbye to John. I feel like I'm dying, again, but I can hold on. I can do this for Roman because I guess I owe him too. Even though I did think he was about to kill me. He still might with that bloody thermometer. I do care about him. Do I? I must. If I didn't, would he not be dead by now? Or wait, is it the other way around? I need his companionship.

I'm dying. I'm not going to disrespect John by interrupting this ceremony. I will not although Roman to take me anywhere.
"Roman. Go. I am asking you to go and say goodbye to him from me. This is the last chance you will have; don't let yourself regret not saying goodbye when you had the opportunity. I don't want to put you through that, you numpty. Go or watch me wallow. I'm not going anywhere, am I? I'll still be here."
"Okay. I'll be right back when it's done okay. I love you. Please don't die on me. Don't die."
"I don't think I have a choice over that but I

Darkness

will be fine for the moment. I l..lo..love you
too. Now go, you doofus."

He bends down and puts his hand on the back of
my head, just above my cut. He places his lips
against mine. He places his bottom lip in my
mouth and I place my top lip in his mouth. We
just stay like that for a few moments. When he
finally pulls away, he just wipes my forehead.
"I swear, I will be back as soon as I can. I'll
get something for the hyperpyrexia."

He walks out of the door.
I'll be fine. I mean, I've only got blood
poisoning; I've come back from worse.

Well I say that...

Darkness

Chapter 17

My temperature keeps changing. From as cold as
ice to as hot as hell. It goes through shifts. I
can't find a constant temperature. Hyperpyrexia
is a bitch. I can feel my heart beating out of
my chest. Boom, boom, boom, boom, boom...boom,
boom. The world is spinning again. This is hell.
Physical hell. Internal biological warfare.
At least I could pass out from the pain. I feel
nauseous and sweaty and disorientated.

I take my shirt and jeans off. Naively believing
I will get any form of relief from it. I can't
walk but I can move. If I can move, I can
attempt to cool myself. Aw, he left a bucket by
the side of the bed. It's nice to know he cares.
Of course he cares.

I said I loved him.
Do I love him?
After everything he's done for me, how can I not

love him? He's perfect for me. The water to my
fire. He's the moth to my flame. Why would I
inflict my love upon him right now? When my
mortality is in question? Is that cruel or kind?
Reciprocation or emotional brutality?

There is only one truth to this. I am not
emotionally void towards him. But I am dying. I
can feel it. The fire pulsing through my veins.
The bacteria's toxin invading every inch of my
body. My bloodstream turning against me. My own
defences attacking my own blood. As I said
before, biological warfare and I can feel it. I
can feel each bullet being fired. Each casualty.

I can hear something outside. The flames. It's
begun. There's no turning back now. He's gone. I
mean, he was gone already but now...damn. After
this, ash will be all that is left of him. It
reminds me of the legend of the phoenix, another
story from John, where the phoenix is born again
from the ash.

However, to rise it must first face purification
by fire. It must be burn to be reborn. I think
he told me about that so I wouldn't be scarred
when I watched them burn a stillborn baby. No
wonder I'm messed up.

They're singing now. He hated singing. He
thought it was pointless. As if song was going

to do anything for them. It's not going to please them, they're dead. They're singing Amazing Grace. Oh he would murder them if he could hear them. He always hated that song. That bloody song. I would always sing it to piss him off and he would piss me off by saying I had a nice voice.

It's actually quite sweet. It's like a knock off choir. I can make out Roman's voice. He's the loudest of them. He has a baritone voice. His last act of defiance to John. Singing at his burning ceremony. I could almost laugh. John would have laughed to hear it. This isn't the way it should be. He should be scrutinising another funeral. This is so wrong. The say only the good die young but that isn't entirely true. Our experiences determine who we are. Some need to be baptised in fire before their greatness can be understood. John wasn't a good man. He was a great man but never a good man. There is a difference. If his loses hadn't been so great, he could have been a good man, a moral man. He was willing to do what it takes and that's why I will always admire him.

Abruptly, everything changes. I can't move. I can't move anything. I can't breathe, I can't blink, I can't see. My eyes have rolled up into my head. I think I'm having a seizure. I begin to choke. I'm choking on my own tongue.

Darkness

Everything is becoming so blurred. My body is spasming. I have lost all control of my limbs. I feel like a fish out of water, flapping around. If I can't stop myself choking, I'm going to knock myself out, best case scenario. Either that or I am going to die. There is no best case scenario. Where's Roman? I shouldn't of let him leave me. Of course, I would knock on death's door again during the cremation of a father figure.

I'm just going to have to run this seizure out. I can't breathe.
I'm going to pass out again.

"Lex? Lex! God, no. Come on, I leave you alone for five minutes. Rita, she's turning blue. Do they actually do that? Oh god, help her! Don't just stand there, this is your department! If she dies Rita, I will never forgive you."

I can't open my eyes but I can hear him. This scenario again. I'm trapped inside my body again. I've passed out, I know that. I can feel my limbs are still flailing. I'm still having a seizure. How long is this bloody seizure. I'm going blue. Cool, like one of those X-Men. No, not cool. Blue means no oxygen in the blood. No oxygen in the blood means death. I'm dying. You can tell my brain's being deprived of oxygen.

Darkness

"She's tachycardic, hyperpyrexia and she does
have septicaemia. Damn, Roman if you're going to
be over emotional, leave. You're not helping her
by being here. Make yourself useful. You're the
one who let her go, remember that. You will not
blame me if she dies, you will blame yourself.
Now go. Find me some Prontosil. You're wasting
time staring at me. Go you silly git!"

She has no right to say that to him. Everything
that I have done has been my choice. It has
nothing to do with Roman or her or the children.
It has always been my choice and I will not have
my death on his conscience. He's a good man who
doesn't deserve that weight on his shoulders. I
will not be his burden.

It's not the same as before. There's no vivid
colours or imaginary mother waiting at the end.
There is just darkness but the sound. The sound
is deafening. I can hear everything around me. I
mean everything. I can hear the flicker of the
flame. The flapping of butterfly wings. I know I
have good hearing but not that good. Why can I
hear all of this? It's too loud. Can a sound be
vivid? Will my next near death experience have
strong tastes? Pungent odours?

If I can think, I'm alive. The brain is the last
thing to die. How reassuring.
Should I be worried that I can't think?

Darkness

It takes a few attempts to open my eyes. It feels like they've been sealed shut. I feel like I've gone blind. I would make a joke of it if I was sure I'm not. I'm frightened. I've never had a seizure like that. I've never even had a seizure before. I never want to go through that again.

Roman is waiting at the end of the end of the bed with a needle. He looks half crazed. He doesn't look like he's slept in days. I feel bad for taking so long to come around. I can't remember much about it. I just know I never want to go through it again. He jabs the needle into my foot, not looking. I wince. He looks me in the eye and rushes to the head of the bed.

"Lex, can you hear me? You've been out for a week. You had a seizure. You've been on a course of Prontosil everyday to try and remove the infection. The fact you're awake is proof you may be okay. I'd better get Rita."
I grab hold of the bottom of his shirt. It's not enough to stop him moving but enough to say what I want to express. I know what I'm scared of. I'm unnerved by the darkness. I'm terrified of it and I never thought I would be. Turns out choking on your own tongue and saliva will do that to you.

Darkness

He places his lips against my mouth with
aggression, as if he is hungry for my flesh. I
reciprocate in kind. I want to feel him. I know
what I want. I want him. Who knows being oxygen
deprived would make you so horny?

He begins to trace the line down my neck and
kissing each point. He picks me up, keeping his
lips on mine. Once he gets me back to his room,
I know what's going to happen. I'm about to drop
my v-card. Do I care? Yes. Am I scared? Yes. Am
I willing to do this? Yes.

I am already in my bra and knickers so that
makes the job easier. He moves his lips down my
body, from my neck to my stomach. I undo my bra
and he begins to kiss and suck on my breasts.
This is weird but I like it. What the hell? I
blame it on the oxygen deprivation.

I let out an involuntary groan. He then moves
back up to my face and kisses me again. I suck
on his bottom lip and bite it gently. He
responds by placing his tongue inside my mouth
and I respond in kind. French kissing, I like
it.

I look down at his groin. He has a boner. He
gets up on the bed and I help him undo his jeans
and he chucks them on the floor. Not looking

where they land. He then takes his boxers off.
It's nothing I haven't seen before. Not too bad.
"Are you sure you want to do this? I understand
if you don't."
I nod.

He then lays on top of me trying to get inside
me. It only takes him two tries but I feel it
when he does, it feels strange. Every human
instinct is guiding me. I mean humans are
animals. Our only purpose is to procreate. I
just let my animalistic urges control me. He
gazes into my eyes. I can see nothing but lust
and passion. He bend his head down to kiss me on
the lips again, only this time he's more gentle.
He begins to thrust and that is when I feel it.
Ow. They always so your first time is painful
but ow. It's a different kind of pain. It stings
which forces me to grit my teeth. It's a
pleasurable pain, it keeps me wanting more. He
continues to thrust, getting faster each time.
This feels like ecstasy. I don't even know how
to describe. I feel truly alive. So does he by
the sounds he's making.

So that was an orgasm. Why have I waited so
long? God. He rolls onto the bed next to me and
pants. Sex. Good exercise. We look at each other
and burst out giggling. Did we just do that? Oh
my god. I am no longer a virgin. Shit. Roman
just kisses me and smiles.

Darkness

"See what you've been missing?"
"Yeah. Wow. Um. Okay then. Did I do okay? You
know, laying down."
"Yeah. You were perfect. You are perfect," he
kisses my neck again "was it okay? For you? I
didn't hurt you or anything did I?"
"Yes, I'm fine. That was really...something. So
I'm alive then?"
"I hope you are. I'm not into necrophilia. So
you're okay? That's surprising because we didn't
use a condom. It usually hurts like hell the
first time, without a condom."
"I wouldn't worry about me being pregnant; I
haven't had my period for the past two months.
Yeah, it didn't hurt that badly. Strange, isn't
it?"
"No. You're still asleep."

"What? I'm sorry. What the hell?"
I haven't woke up. But...but...so that wasn't
real. None of that was real. I don't know
whether to be disappointed or not. Oh god. What
the hell?
"Did I stutter? You haven't woken up yet. This
is all inside your head, you little pervert. I'm
sure Roman would be flattered to find out he's
the subject of your wet dreams. I mean come on,
do you think he would be such a dominant lover?
He's a sap. Didn't you wonder why you did break
your hymen?

Darkness

No, you're still asleep. Sorry to break it to
you my dear."

What the hell?
I wasn't...that was...huh?
Everything that just happened. That couldn't
have been in my imagination. Oh my god. I'm
still unconscious. Damn it.

Well, I'm fucked.
Literally and metaphorically.

Chapter 18

I am still unconscious. I don't know whether to
be embarrassed about having a wet dream over
Roman; who knew I am so sexually frustrated?

It was so...vivid.
I have no idea if I preferred the sweet
stereotypical idea of the moment before death or
if I preferred the passionate sexual frustration
I seemed to exhibit. Did I really believe that
was real? Of course I wanted to feel alive
because I was dying and still am. It makes so
much sense. Roman wouldn't take that risk if I
was recovering from septicaemia. I wouldn't be
so chirpy if I had just woken up after a week
out. I guess I was too 'caught up' in the heat
of the moment. The imaginary moment, granted but
wow. If sex is anything like that in reality,

take me now. But then again, everything went the way I wanted. It's in my head after all.

If I could wake up any moment now, that would be great. Not that I don't love being trapped in my thoughts and in the sickness that is my mind but if I could wake up, I would be grateful. I don't know to whom I'd be grateful. Myself?

I can feel a pin prick. I can't identify where but I can feel which is an advantage. Physical pain, amazing for clarity am I right? I am still frightened. So, run down on septicaemia. Let's Sherlock Homes this bitch. The infection can't have been incubating for two weeks otherwise, the symptoms would have presented themselves earlier. Would I have not noticed if my wound was infected? Wouldn't Rita have noticed? I mean it hurt, the injury, but after the trauma to the body, that is natural. Maybe the infection lead to the sepsis. No, it takes just a matter of hours to materialise or for the infection to take hold.

Wait. There's another injury I hadn't considered. I have this cut on my hip. I don't know how I got it but maybe that's to blame. No. It has to be my bullet wound. It has to be. It was always a risk that it could become infected; it was difficult to know but that what this has to be. Staphylococcus. It happens.

Darkness

I'm done, I need to wake up.
I can only deduce so much. I could be a mini
Sherlock. Because after all, it's elementary. Oh
Sherlock Holmes quotes, never get old. Anyone
who disrespects those novellas deserves to burn
in hell-fire. That's just my impartial view on
this.

The infection. The actual infection that wiped
out the drips of humanity. It's complicated to
describe I guess. It starts off like a flu type
thing; you begin to cough and your sinuses
become painful. It's easy to mistake it for flu
or sinusitis. I guess it is a form of influenza.
There is only one thing can is similar and that
was the outbreak of Spanish Influenza in 1918.
Apparently, it devastated the Western world. It
was a pandemic. It wiped out more people than
the first world war and the Black Death of 1347
to 1351.

100 million were wiped out worldwide in a single
year. It's nothing when you compare it to 5
billion in two years, or that's what was
predicted.

The virus the continues to give you respiratory
issues; it gets harder to breathe. That's the
blood building up and solidifying as a mass. The
irritation through coughing causes bleeding in

the throat. Blood begins to build up in the
lungs, acting as a form of pneumonia. This can
cause the lung to collapse, best case scenario.

It is a painful demise. It continues to build up
until you begin to suffocate. Blood begins to
flow from every orifice. If you die at this
point, you're lucky. Believe it or not, this is
the least painful and quickest part.

If your pain continues, if you survive having
blood flowing out of every part, you will then
begin to experience delirium, paranoia and
hallucinations. Mental disintegration. Once
insanity takes hold, your organs will shut down
meaning that you will experience jaundice, renal
failure, followed by a major heart attack. After
that, death.

You see why, in their case, euthanasia is the
kindest option. You need to identify it early.
On top of the fast progression of the disease,
it is incredibly contagious. Hence why most of
the population was wiped out when they were all
in such close proximity to each other.
Does that aid your understanding? Of this world?
The main threat. That's what you're always told.
The virus. The virus is the big bad but they
warm you about human violence. Gun shots, stab
wounds, strangulation, overdose. It's always
about disease.

Darkness

In some ways, it's easy to relate to the virus. It's dead but it just wants to be alive. It uses human cells, corrupts them, just to feel and to be alive. It's that what we all want, to be alive?
Unless you're suicidal. In which case, that's not the aim.

But it's always sod's law. Those who want to survive die and those who want to die survive. If there is a God, he has a love for irony but then again, I would. If I had control over a planet, I'd torture the little bastards. I think everyone would. Looking at these little monkeys that fall out a tree and invent the digital watch yet think they have a right to make themselves gods. Dictating over life and death. They'd deserve everything they get. One thing humanity has in common with deities. A desire to punish those who believe themselves to be superior.
My favourite example of that is Hitler. There were three opportunities when he could have died and yet, only his own bullet could end him. A coward's end for the puppeteer. I hope he resides in hell. Burning as he forced millions to burn. John taught us a lot of things and that was one of them. Our history defines us. It is so easy to want people to suffer but you become inhuman when you take pleasure in losing your

Darkness

humanity.

I'm bored now.
I think about a lot of things but it's maddening
when you are alone with your thoughts because
you can contemplate everything. Every second
feels like a year. A year alone with your
thoughts. I would definitely need a
straitjacket.

I can feel a squeezing sensation. What the hell?
I hope my hands being squeezed otherwise I will
bitch slap someone. This time I can't respond. I
can't hear anything. I can't even identify where
I'm being touched. Am I paralysed? I'm not too
clued up on if septicaemia can cause full body
paralysis but if I'm paralysed, that's game
over. They all know that's what I'd want. Rita
could do it. She's done it to younger people
than me. It's the reason she is so damaged,
internally and externally.

Abruptly, something changes. I can actually feel
my blood pumping. I can hear my heart beating at
the speed of sound. Adrenaline. It was only a
matter of time before they got the hint. But
wait...they only administer adrenaline if the
heart stops. Did my heart stop? Is that why I
could hear nothing? Oh my god, that's a contrast
to the last time.

Darkness

Maybe my heart didn't stop. Maybe my body is trying to fight back. Who knew a hormone could be the thing to revitalise a person? I just have to fight again. My body working with me. My body against infection. Pretty cool. If that's the case.
Maybe the adrenaline is pumping due to my little...hm...wet dream. Do you release adrenaline when you do the deed? I have no idea; complete virgin, I can't be blamed. Can't be judged. Whenever I have a 'simple' moment, I can know blame it on oxygen deprivation. Not that I'm bright anyway but I know how to survive. Okay, maybe not. That would be ironic. Okay, I will come to a compromise with my title. I am amazing at surviving if I do not have a bullet hole in me or I am in aseptic conditions, with a lack of pathogens around me. Yeah, sums it up.

Now I can feel the pain again. Right, I just have to work with my body. Okay. Right. I have my heart rate on my side and the adrenaline. I can feel sensations more vividly. Pinpricks. Squeezing. Ah. Oh my god. The pain begins to consume me yet again. Only living things feel pain. Only living things feel pain. Am I even alive or is this an illusion as well? A sick illusion but an illusion all the same, am I wrong?

I feel a building pressure in my chest. I don't

know what I need to do to relieve it. Cough or breathe? I don't know. My chest feels like it is about to explode. I feel like I'm suffocating again. I can hear strangled noises escaping from my throat. I want to claw at my neck. If there was a hole in my neck, I would be able to breathe. The pressure might go away. I want to do all of these things but I can't.

I can hear. It seems blocked, as if my ears are blocked. It sounds like I'm underwater. It's hard to determine anything that does sound like I'm surrounded by goldfish blubbing at me. That is a disturbing image, just massive human sized fish staring at you. That's enough to put a kid in therapy for the next ten years. Then again, if that was enough to put someone into therapy, I would need to signed up for at least fifty years worth. We all would.

I suddenly jolt up, gasping. I'm back. Back to Earth with a bang. The pressure seems to be alleviated. I collapse back down, keeping my eyes open. I can see Roman and Rita at my sides. Roman does look sleep depraved but not like the Lothario in my vision. I look down at my arm. There's an IV drip in my arm with some form of saline solution in it. Maybe not saline. Maybe Prontosil but where would they have found a magic bullet?

Darkness

"Lex. Lex. Calm down, okay. Everything will be fine I promise, won't it Rita? We're going to kill this bloody infection, okay."
"Yes, don't worry. Okay, worry. You died for two minutes. Heart stopped. You were technically dead but now you're alive, so there could be damage to the brain."

Aren't you just the voice of comfort and light Rita, you bitch. So I died...that's nice to know. How can I not panic? That's like telling a baby not to cry. I actually died. How the bloody hell did that happen? I mean really. It was so different than last time. Maybe that was for good reason.

I still feel disorientated but I can't quite remember what happened before the haze. That's what they say; you can't remember having a seizure but then again, my brain cells are frazzled as they are. I don't need help screwing myself up anymore than I already am.
The world is spinning.

If I can just keep my eyes open, maybe this will begin to make sense. This bullshit may finally begin to make sense because my mind's made up. I've made my choice and it is impossible to convince me otherwise. I have to find out who I am. Who I really am. I need to find my parents, if they are still alive. I need to find out why

Darkness

John stole me from my parents, there must have been a reason. There always is. They didn't abandon me. They didn't abandon me? I mean, I am so confused.

Why do I remember waking up alone, scared and freezing? Why do I remember having to fend for myself for a few days? Why can't I remember my past for what it was? My parents could have lived for ten years, thinking I was dead. Do they think I'm dead, if they're still alive? Do my parents think they have a dead daughter? Do I have brothers? Sisters?

All of my life I have been trying to figure out the mystery that is my past. That cold, dark void in my mind that needs to be illuminated. I owe it to myself to find out the truth behind it all. I have to find the truth from the only ones who know. The one place I should belong.

I need to unravel the riddle that is my past. My first step towards finally living.

How can I even consider finding other survivors when I don't know who I really am?

Darkness

Chapter 19

I've slept a lot the past four days. The
Prontosil is taking it out of me. Rita said they
would but it is just exhausting being tired.
Elektra, title stating the bleeding obvious.

I just need to be alone.
I'm stubborn and once I'm set on something, I
will not relent. I have to find them. My
parents, if they're even still alive. What if
I've been denied closure on my parents for the
past ten years? A decade not being able to piece
things together. I have to find some form of
closure; some form of purpose that gives my life
a real meaning. An opportunity for me to belong
to something bigger than this. After all, blood
is thicker than water.

Darkness

All I remember from the last four days is having
IV tubes inserted into my arms and legs, trying
to stave the infection off but I've been too out
of it. Not the typical drug fuelled haze, but
more of a contemplative state. I finally have a
goal to work towards. I've made up my mind and
this time, nothing is going to stop me. Not even
Roman.

I need to know the truth behind who I really am.
Before I die, I have to know this. I have to.
There is no choice anymore. Even if I don't find
them, at least I'm getting away: allowing myself
time to think and contemplate things.

I guess dying bring out the thinker in me. I
still feel disorientated but my eyes are
beginning to allow me to see things as they
really are again. I've tried getting up but I've
had to move around attached to bags of saline
and liquid antibiotics. I think I'm becoming
desensitised to everything. Nothing feels like
it has an effect anymore.

"Hey Lex, how are you feeling? You're definitely
looking better, getting your colour back."
My colour is back. Is that the only indication
of my health that he could identify?
"I feel like shit but how are you?"
I readjust my position so I am leaning on my

elbows. Every one of my joints creak as I do this but I'm just going to have to deal with it; when you don't use them for a while, they rust up. Did I just compare myself to the bloody tin man? Maybe.

He smiles.
"You look a million time better than you feel, I assure you. You are so beautiful Lex, I don't think you know just how gorgeous you are."
"I am not and you didn't answer my question. Rita still giving you hell?"
"Yeah. She is becoming a proper bitch. Just because I told her not to come near sick people with a cigarette in her hand and she makes me out to be the bad guy. Ugh. Not everyone wants lung cancer, like her."

It's odd to see Roman so pissed at someone. He just flares his nostrils but keeps his voice at the same tone. If you couldn't see him, you'd think he was calm. He just goes really red and his nostril flare. Not like me. I just go really red, my voice becomes high pitched and I develop a bloodshot eye. I know, weird right.

"She needs a cigarette, Roman. She's out of order but she's under a lot of pressure. Do you want me to have a word with her? Tell her to ease off because I mean, I have nothing but time."

Darkness

"I can fight my own battles, Lex. But if you could, I wouldn't object to it."

That's codename for 'Lex, please help me because Rita scares the crap out of me'. I've come to learn this. What he needs is someone to stand up for him, even though he is older than the rest of us. I'm not sure if that's cowardice or bravery.

"I'll talk to her about it when she comes in to give me my drugs. After, not before. She will 'accidentally' give me too much arsenic or something."
"Yeah, she probably would. Well, good luck." He kisses me on the cheek and begins to bolt for the door.
"You are unbelievable, you know that, you dickhead."
"I know."

He is such a cock sometimes, I swear. I'm not sure if me confronting Rita in regards to her smoking habit in a time of stress is brave or stupid. Then again, aren't they the same thing? To be brave is to be stupid enough to take the risks that others will not. Can I afford to take this risk? You know because she has the drugs and can make my death look like an accident.

Darkness

Poor git. I do feel sorry for him; he always has such a hard time. Everyone does but I understand what it's like to feel the pressure of expectations. I just ran instead of facing it like he did. Crap, footsteps. Moment of truth.

"Rita, light of my life, how are you? Are you well?"
"What do you want Elektra? You only ask me how I am when you want something."
"You should probably give me the drugs right about now. I want my drugs. Why do you always think I have an ulterior motive?"
"Because you do. You do always want something."

She inserts a needle into the catheter attached to the saline solution. She inserts another needle into my arm and I feel the relief flow through my blood like a river. Do I have to tell her?

She then places herself in the arm chair and takes a roll up out of her pocket. She also takes out a pack of Swan matches.
"Right, I've given you the drugs," she clenches the roll up between her teeth and strikes the match. She lights it and draws a breath from it. "Now, you talk."

I feign a cough. I hate the smell of cigarette smoke; it clings to everything. The walls and

Darkness

curtains. It clings like yellow fingers. Similar
to the smoker's fingers. I don't want to have to
tell her; she knows the rules. You do not smoke
in the house. Not in front of the kids in a box
like configuration. She's never done that before
but why is she doing it now? She's all we have
now. She can't give up on us now.

"You've been smoking like a chimney. Inside.
Where the kids are. You've been giving Roman a
really hard time about things. I just want
answers."

She exhales and a cloud of mist is released. She
doesn't even look at me but at the silent
assassin in her hand. She puts the cigarette
into her mouth and sucks another breath.
She exhales again.

"You want answers? I don't know how I'm supposed
to deal with this shit storm. I have done
everything to keep this bloody camp safe and
what do I get in return; John goes and off's
himself. I am done, Elektra. Done."
She draws again. She exhales the smoke into my
face.
If I wasn't incapacitated, I would have punched
her. I don't care, she has no right to be such a
bitch. We all lost John and the rest of us
haven't fallen apart, wallowing in self pity.
She was doing this even before he died. How dare

193

Darkness

she blame this on him?

"Rita, I'm going to cut the crap. Pull yourself together. You have a responsibility to the group and if you shirk that, you will have more blood on your hands than you can bear. Now, put the cigarette out and get some air."
"No, I will not be told what to do by you, you ungrateful little slut."

I reach forward, snatching the cigarette from her hand. What the hell am I supposed to do with it? So I make an impulsive decision. I want to leave anyway. I owe her retaliation for her blowing smoke into my face. I stub the cigarette out...on her arm. I am so dead now.

She winces in pain.
"You evil little bitch!"
That's when she punches me square in the nose. I hear the crack. She's broken my nose. The bitch. I liked my nose.
I can taste the blood that's flowing out of my nose. I can't breathe. Which way do they say to tilt your head? Forward. Let it rush out. If you put your head back, there's the possibility to choke on your blood. I let my head tip forward naturally. I'm going to kill her. She comes anywhere near me again, a burnt arm will be the least of her worries. That's not a threat, that's a promise.

Darkness

She walks out of the room, observing her arm to
see if anything else would develop. I have to
get out of here now. I am definitely not staying
if that maniacal bitch is in charge. I am done
with all of this bullshit. I try to be
reasonable and I end with a broken nose.

I shift towards the edge of the bed. I just have
to get the blood flow into my legs. Oh shit.
That's not the only place where there's blood
flow.
Really, did I have to start my period now? After
all this time? It's like Mother Nature's way of
saying 'congratulation, another month and you're
still not pregnant. Your reward, bleed for a
week and survive'.

I just have to get up and deal with it. I
hoarded a supply of tampons. Why did it have to
start now? Couldn't have made an appearance at
any other time when I'm not hatching an escape
plan.

My legs are Bambi like but I can still do it. I
go over to the edge of the room and retrieve my
rucksack but then I realise. I have to get some
new clothes; these ones are covered in blood. I
just have to get up the stairs but first, it
would help if I detached myself from the many IV
drips attached to me. It stings but I'm too

hyped up now. My nose is still bleeding but I could really care less.

I have to pull myself up the stairs; my legs are too weak to carry me up them but the white stair carpet now has a nice streak of red through the middle. Oh and also bloody hand prints.

I run into my room. I have about five minutes to get my crap together and get the hell out of dodge. Do I take Roman with me? No, I have to focus on getting myself out of here. I swear if she comes near me, I will kill her. I stand by what I said. What I've always said. If she gets sick, I will kill. I never specified what kind of sick. Mentally sick is included; I was just waiting for her to crack.

They need him here. To keep things in order. He was built for this kind of life, protecting people. He'll do well. I just have to live for myself right now.

I grab a load of shirts and jeans. Only three of each. I'll have time to clean them while I'm on the road; I have my plan of action. I take my trousers and shirt off. It takes a bit of effort to peel them off; I'll just have to leave them. It's a good thing the previous occupant of this room had such a love of ironic t-shirts that I don't think have ever been funny. Like what the

Darkness

joke about a pug with large glasses with a hash-
tag 'selfie'. What the hell is a selfie?

I put that shirt on. I have to change my
underwear. I grab all of the pairs I have and
change into a black pair. I have a sanitary
towel on so I shouldn't have to worry about that
for a few hours. I put on a pair of mud crusted
jeans, the first to hand. It is still an
endeavour to slide them on because everytime I
bend forward, I feel like my brain is about to
disintegrate and fall out through my nose.
Apparently that's what the Egyptians used to do
to their dead, isn't it? Hook their brain out
and pull it through their noses. That is some
nasty shit right there.

I just need my lace up walking boots. They are
caked in mud but they are the most comfortable
shoes I own and that's what I have to consider.
My fingers aren't nimble enough to tie the laces
at a sufficient speed. I'm wasting too much
time, reinventing the bloody wheel. Fiddling
while Rome burns. Faffing about. Ah, the joys of
British slang.

I steal a glance of myself in the mirror.
I do look like crap. I am stupidly pale and
sickly looking. My hair falls across my face
like a haystack. My nose appears slightly
crooked but my entire face is smeared with

blood. If my torso didn't look brutal enough, I now have a broken nose to match my cut lip. I can see the beginnings of a black eye; who knew the bitch packed such a heavy punch?

I have to run. I have to. I just have to sneak into the cupboard, get a few medical supplies, and I'm set. I am so close. I had to bring my plans forward but I'm actually going to do it.

I slide down the stairs on my arse which I haven't done since I was a child. I am trying to make as little noise as possible; I have to get away from here and I am not spending another second with her. I saw her as a mentor? I wouldn't trust her with a guinea pig. She's always had someone there to help her, she has no real talent of her own. She may be in her element with a scalpel in her hand but that does not mean it's the best thing for the poor sod underneath her knife.

I leg it for the cupboard. Bandages. Disinfectant. Sutures. Needles and surgical thread. Okay, I should be fine with that. I can hear her breathing. I think most of London could. A strained breath.

She's puffing on another cigarette. Cursing at me. She hasn't noticed me yet because she's too busy applying ointment to her burn. It was tiny;

Darkness

at least I didn't break her nose.

I take my old leather jacket from the rack. John said he found me with it; it must have been my father's. It was so large it entombed me the first time I tried it on. Now, it's slightly too long but it's sufficient for its purpose. It is black leather. The signs of ageing are present upon it but it still looks kick ass. This was the beginning connection to my family. Well, my parents. I place the rucksack over my back, trying to avoid the items colliding.

I open the door.
I'm free. One more step and I am free for now. I have to go now or I never will. If I stay, I will kill Rita and leave Roman to clear it all up. How can I do that? It's better I leave with as little blood on my hands as possible. Well, I already have enough of my own blood on my hands and I don't need any more.

So I run. I run as fast as I can which is still limited. My lungs are burning from the sensations of the air and anaerobic endurance. I am so nearly there. No time for goodbyes or short comings. I am doing this. I have to. I've cut all ties.

All ties but one.
"Lex."

Darkness

Darkness

Chapter 20

I should have anticipated this, I guess. I don't
look back; I just have to get far enough away
and he might get bored. He has to stay. He has
to stay to protect them otherwise they are
royally screwed.

"Lex, wait!"
I'm not responding. He has to go back.
I can hear him running even faster, his breath
on the back of my neck. He then puts his hand on
my arm and spins me around to face him. He is
panting and red faced. He just stares at me, his
eyes swimming with tears.
"Were you just going to leave without saying

goodbye?"
I look down at his arm.
"Let go of me Roman."
I try to pull away but not before noticing that
my nose is still bleeding; yeah, it probably
would, wouldn't it you bloody idiot. Broken
noses tend to do that.

"What the hell happened? I'm guessing Rita
didn't take to kindly to it but what happened to
make you want to run? We don't run, we fight or
we die. You can't run from this Lex."
"I won't ask you again. Let. Me. Go." I struggle
even more pulling away from him.

He relinquishes his grip, almost defeated. He
looks back at the base and inhales deeply.
"So, where are we going?"
"We are not going anywhere. I am. This doesn't
concern you Roman. I am not staying in that
place; John was the only reason I was planning
on hanging around but now, I have things to take
care of. You have to stay, I can take care of
myself."

I continue walking forward.

"Last time I heard that, you got shot. I am not
letting you out of my sight Lex. Rita will be
fine looking after the kids. How many times do I
need to tell you? You matter more to me than

anything and I will not lose you again."

I pause and I think he notices because his breathing seems to relax again. Why does he feel like it's his job to save me? It isn't his place. I don't want him to be the knight in shining armour. I just have to do this on my own so why is he making this so difficult for me?

"She isn't in her right mind. She will hurt the kids if she isn't supervised. People will die so someone needs to be there to make sure she doesn't murder the children. Roman, you have to stay and I have to go. It's just the way it has to be and you won't stop me."

He looks crestfallen.
There is one thing I can rely on and that is that Roman will not stop until he gets what he wants. He doesn't want to stay, genuinely. Why can't he accept the fact that if he comes with me, the well being of the camp will be compromised. In contrast, there is part of me that wants to let him. It's selfish but protection is what I want. But I don't want it. Ugh!

"Fine. Leave if you want but I will come with you. Look at me and tell me you don't want me with you and I will go. I won't bother you or try to come after you. Just tell me that and I will let you go. Lex?"

I look him in the eyes. I want to tell him that
I want him there with me, to be with me every
step of the way but I have to face the truth.
The truth.

"I don't want you with me. You're a liability.
You wanted the truth and I am giving it to you.
Now go. Don't make it anymore difficult than it
has to be. Just go."

My voice cracks on the final word. I try to
compose myself once again. I can't think of
myself. This is my war, not his. I'm not getting
him involved in this.

He just stands there, blinking at me. He wasn't
expecting me to actually say it. I have shocked
him. I feel obnoxious and vile. He thought I was
a cold bitch before but now, I think I have
excelled myself.

"You're bullshitting me, I can tell. I need your
permission to leave; I don't need your
permission to walk to the same place. You need
me more than you care to admit."

He holds my hand again and pushes me in front of
him; I struggle again, trying to not to move my
feet. I focus all of my abdominal strength into

my feet, stopping myself from moving. However, he still manages to overpower me and just scoops me into his arms and lays me over his shoulder. I start kicking my legs; I feel one of my kicks landing on its mark in the centre of his ribs. I feel him being winded but he still continues. I then involve my arms, punching him in the back like a fleshy punching bag.

"Let me go you bastard! Let me go, let me go, let me go!"
"No, we have things to discuss but first, we have to find a place to lie low for a while and if you keep kicking me, I will drop you on your head."
"You wouldn't dare."
"Oh, try me."

I relent in my physical violence. I'm still warn out from the blood poisoning. He's just as stubborn as am I so it will be impossible to stop him once he is set on something. Why does he want to discuss things? It doesn't concern him. None of this does.

"Now, that's better isn't it? I'm not getting kicked in the back and you get to reserve your energy. I know a little place we can talk about the plan of action; if you need to sleep, feel free."

Darkness

I hadn't thought about it before. I am tired. I am exhausted. My energy reserves have been seriously depleted. I let my eyes close as the sun blares over the horizon.

When I wake up, I feel odd. The room is obscured by a sense of decay. It stinks of tobacco and damp. The walls are covered in mould and the corners are consumed by damp. Dust seems to cover everything; every inch is being conquered by dead skin cells.

"You're awake. I said you could have a sleep; I didn't anticipate you having a full eight hours. Now, why are you running? Second, where are you running to? And third, why did Rita break your nose and give you two black eyes?"

I feel groggy but I still pull myself up. I have to be honest. If I'm honest, he might finally understand why I want to be in solitude.

"First, I am running because I have been planning to for months. Rita just gave me the excuse that I needed. Second, I have no cocking clue. I just have to get away. Three, I told her what she was doing was wrong, she got pissy and I may have stubbed her cigarette onto her arm. Anything else?"

"Fair enough. You think that you're the only one

that she's hurt. Except it wasn't so much the physical kind of violence; actually, maybe it was. But you see the difference between you and me, I have never run. I have never turned away after one incident. I have dealt with it and moved on. Why do you always run?"

"I run because that's what I know! That's what John taught me. Run or die! Don't question me because you have no idea who I am. You don't know me, you're just infatuated with what you want me to be. What the hell are you talking about? Hurt you? Yeah right."

I shouldn't be saying this. He doesn't deserve this but I cannot stop until he leaves and forgets about me. He will in time. I'm sure I'll forget about him eventually and move on with my life. She wouldn't hurt him; she wouldn't. He's just bullshitting me to make me go back with him. I know his bleeding martyr act too well and it doesn't take me in. Hell, I taught him the art of being a bleeding martyr.

"Don't talk about you know nothing about! I am not infatuated with you, I don't particularly like you. I love you. I love you more than I have loved anyone; why do you always push me away? Why do you feel you have to push everyone away? I want to be there for you because you need us. You need me."

The audacity of him. I don't need him. I want
him but I don't need him. I don't need anyone.
He doesn't love me and I don't know how many
times I can say it.

"Lex, you want to know what she did to me? She
touched me. When I was helping her with the
drugs, she would touch my cock and she would
force herself on me. I guess she...raped me.
Yeah, she did. Didn't give me a broken nose but
she still hurt me. Yet I stayed. I stayed for
you, to protect you. So this is my fight and I
am coming with you. I am not staying there if
you aren't."

What the hell is he going on about?
Rita...raping him. I mean I would have seen
unless it started recently. Is he genuinely sick
enough to make up lies like that up about her? I
don't know what to believe but his intentions
are clear as anything. He is trying to put me on
a guilt trip; make me feel like I am a coward
because I run away from something so minor. But
why would he lie about that?

"I don't need you! Why do you not get the
message? Fuck off back to the group. I don't
need your bullshit on top of my own; I have to
do something on my own and if I die, I die. I
don't need you and I don't want you with me.

Darkness

Accept that abode that Erin found if you don't want to go back *there!*"

He looks crestfallen. I think I'm finally getting through to him. I just have to find other survivors and I guess, one day, I might come back. But I am never going to know until I take the plunge into the unknown.

"You know what, screw it. Do what you want. I'm going back and so will you once you come to your senses. Thank you for setting me straight before I really fell for you. Thank you for giving me the clarity to see you for what you really are. Goodbye Elektra."

He hates me.
I can see the venom in his eyes.
At the end of the day, it is better to be hated than loved.

Darkness

Chapter 21

I walk out of the front door, reflecting on what just happened. I think it is safe to say that I have broken the necessary ties to Roman which I admit, I feel awful about but I had to do it, there was no element of choice to the matter. I just wish I didn't have to leave with him hating my guts.

I never noticed what type of building this was. It must be some form of abandoned warehouse or something because when I step outside, there is a scummy, stagnant river. How far did he walk with me?

I just have to make my way to some form of vehicle. The thing about petrol is it went off about two years in. It loses its volatility which makes it crap as a fuel. I guess that's why it's difficult to travel long distances;

being vulnerable for such a long duration of time.

Who says there is no such thing as coincidence? That the universe is rarely so lazy? I can see a bike; it looks like it's been rusted to hell but it will do. I have only ridden a bike once but you know what they say; once you learn, you never forget. Oh, the humiliation if I can't ride the bike and fall on my arse. I probably deserve but I have a little thing called pride that I would like to hold onto for the long term. On reflection, pride and dignity are interconnected in some ways which means I have diminished pride because let's face it, the dignity ship sailed long ago. Dignity, who needs it?
Well, everyone but that's beyond the point.

I walk up to the bike; it's even worse up close. There is not an inch of the bicycle that is not covered in rust and the beginnings of moss growing upon it. This is what I was saying about the whole pride thing; I have to sit on a bike that is going to squeak like a rodent on speed and look like I am riding a tree reject thing moss mound. I do not know how to describe it but I am not above feeling my arse deserves better than this. But, I have no choice. It doesn't do well to be proud in this world and if this is the only mode of transport, then that is what it

Darkness

is and I have to accept that. Ew, though. Ew.

As I sit down on the seat, the sensation is
awful. I get a sharp feeling on the back of my
legs as a jet of putrefied water escapes. How
many years of rain that lie in that seat...I
don't want to think about. All I know is it
makes me feel like I have pissed myself again
which is not a nice a sensation. The only
difference is that urine is warm, at least, but
this water is bitterly cold and sends a shiver
down my spine. John used to say that when a
shiver went down your spine, that was someone
walking over your grave. I wonder if he feels it
now; someone walking over his ashes. I clear my
throat. Now is not the time to be getting over
emotional. A lot has happened recently but I can
mourn and grieve and all that bullshit once I
get to the final destination. Then, I can mourn
my losses and find out who I really am?
Am I a daughter? A killer?
An amnesiac, sociopath with limited
understanding of the workings of human beings?
I can't be a sociopath. I care too much. Scrap
that, I'm more like a psychopath if we are to be
specific.

It takes a few attempts to get the peddles to
work but once they do, I finally feel like what
I want to achieve is achievable. I have hope
which is something I haven't had for the longest

Darkness

time. Hope. It sounds so bloody fickle but it is
a reality for me now. The world is going to shit
at my feet but at least I have a hope in hell of
achieving something for once.

It's cold. I haven't really had the room in my
mind to comprehend how cold it is. I mean it is
some time in Spring, it must be, but it is
bloody freezing. My jacket continues to be
utterly useless but, and I hate to admit it, it
makes me feel close to something. Sentimentality
I presume. This did used to be my father's, if I
can believe what John said. Can I trust anything
he said? I mean, did he do it for my benefit? To
protect me from a life not worth living? Were my
parents the real villains?

I don't want to think about it. I don't want to
and I can't be arsed to. I can tell I haven't
been on a bike in a while, the burning sensation
in my shins persists in occupying mind space.
Oh, it burns. Like riding the bloody horse, just
a different type of pain. Ha, what a stupid
statement.

The horizon is bleak.
Clouds occupy every inch of the sky; they're
grey like usual. If they were white, that would
be the first indication of snow and I will not
even get into my hatred of that cold, wet,
freezing frozen rain thing. Yet again, not great

213

at describing such things. The weather. The old barometric situation. Meteorological influences. Funny words, am I right? Why are there so many words in the English language to describe just one thing? Why was the weather not just called the weather. Not really anyone I can ask anymore. I think most of the people that made the dictionaries died in the early days. Probably died while running with their dictionary trying to stop their glasses falling off of their little eggheads.
Well, that's what John used to say.

John was mean to the little bodkins because he wasn't one of them. I mean John was a philosophical man, brilliant but ask him how you would create various carboxylic acids and use them to create synthetic esters and...nothing. Nada. No understanding whatsoever.

Side note; if you want to know about carboxylic acids and esters, carboxylic acids are formed when alcohols oxidise. Like when wine goes off and starts to taste like vinegar. If you were to react carboxylic acids with an alcohol in the presence of a sulfuric acid catalyst, it would produce an ester. They can be produced for their smells, naturally occurring esters are found in fruits. Oh yes, not just a hat rack.

There is something quite freeing about riding a

bike. I mean, riding a horse is liberating in
its own way but riding a bike. The wind
fluttering through my hair. The baby hairs on
the back of my head pricking up like the ears of
a feral chihuahua. I am going at quite a speed.
The wind burns my eyes, causing them to water. I
feel like I am blind. I can barely see anything
but this is amazing. I feel free, finally.

I've been riding for hours. I have no idea how
far I have travelled due to the lack of the road
signs. My nose is killing me, my shins ache and
my vagina is on fire. So overall, I am alright.

I bloody hate road signs. The government removed
them all to prevent the movement of people.
People who lived in the countryside were unable
to travel into the major cities and people who
lived in the major cities couldn't travel to the
country. They had no idea of the mileages and
the boundaries of regions changed. The city of
London shrank significantly. The governments
thought that this would aid the containment of
the contagion. Look how brilliantly that turned
out for them.

Nobody could travel. Quarantine in its most
basic form. Nobody infected got out. Nobody
unaffected got in. But like everything, where
there's quarantine or borders, there will always
be people smuggled in or out.

Darkness

John used to live in the heart of London.

"John, come on. I know all of that stuff. Tell me about London. What it was like to live in the city?"
I was always so inquisitive in regards to living in a highly urbanised area. The rush of living in a place where you never see the same face twice. Noise. Cars. Pollution. Life.

"Alright goose, patience. It was bloody awful. The people were obnoxious and do not even get me started on the traffic..."
I interjected, "You know that's not what I mean. Tell me what it was like! You promised!"
"Alright. It was like living in a hub. A hub of life and activity. There was always somewhere to go, a place to belong or die trying.
This place used to be called Blackheath. It was a mass burial site for victims of the Black death in the 1350's. It used to be right on the outskirts of London, just a half an hour train journey from central London. After the disintegration of the town and cities in 2015, it became a part of Kent officially. I lived in central London because my wife was training to become a lawyer and it was close to the Old Bailey. That's why it took us by surprise. The news reports always went on about the sun solar flares getting stronger but why would we believe them? We'd spent millennia at the top of the

Darkness

food chain and yet we believed ourselves to be
above nature; we deserve everything that
happened."

He wiped his brow and looked at me. He knew
everything to say that would piss me off
because, indirectly, he blamed himself and
humanity for natural intervention. He was pining
for sympathy or something like but he knew I
wasn't going to fall for his bullshit. He knew I
didn't want to hear his sob story, I wanted to
know how he escaped from the centre of a
quarantine city with no form of transportation.

"On the 18th of December 2019, I decided it was
time to up and leave. I had lost everything and
I had had to watch my wife suffer and die and I
wasn't allowed to find her a doctor. I had
nothing left to lose but little Isla so the way
ahead was clear. I found one of my friends on
the outside, there may have been no phones but
there was still letter writing. I wrote to him
and we agreed the date; he would bring the car
and I would have someone cause a diversion while
I got myself and Isla into the car. The plan,
fool proof."

I could tell that he was visualising it; he
always had this expression of exasperation and
he let his vision consume him. No one else
existed when he told a story and I guess that

was always why I was so fascinated by him. He
could forget the world just like a normal person
could fall asleep. I envied him. He had a pool
of memories from before; more than any of us
kids had.

"I'm not proud of what I did that day," he said
"I did what I had to to get out. The day came
upon us and I left everything I had. Isla was
still a tiny baby so she had no possessions,
just me. Eugene, my friend with the car, arrived
as planned. He was having his papers checked by
the authorities and he looks shady as hell, I
remember. The car was being monitored. So I
grabbed a hold of this boy, he must have been
sixteen or seventeen. He was coughing his guts
up. So I stabbed him. He was just the diversion
I needed. I stabbed him in the chest so it was
quick but he was the diversion I needed. They
all crowded around him, comforting him. Then I
got in the car and just faded away. That's how I
got away. Is that really what you wanted to
know?"

I remember hating him for months after that. He
had taken a life unnecessarily. John had always
prepared us to fire a gun from the age of
fifteen but never had he told us to use a knife.
He said that if we had to kill, we had to make
it as painless as possible for them. It
shouldn't be murder but euthanasia, like the

Darkness

Lennie situation. I remember I was thirteen when
we had that conversation but it's always been
there at the back of my mind, nibbling away, and
now that he's dead...
I can't help feeling that John didn't have the
right to kill that boy. He could have found
another diversion to just injure him but no, he
murdered him. I guess now I don't have the right
to question him. I have been inside the mind of
a killer and I have to admit...it felt 'right'
to kill that man in the manner that I did. I
sped up the end of his life and made him suffer.
It was either me or him and I am alright with
what I did. In a sick way, I feel like I can
find peace with that. Just like John did.

Did John kill my parents? I hadn't thought about
it before but is that why he took me? He killed
my parents as a diversion and stole me away.
Maybe hit me over the head so I wouldn't
remember? Is that what happened to me?

No. He wouldn't have done that. He wouldn't
deprive a child of their parents but then again,
that is what he did.

I place my hand inside my pocket and take out an
old lighter. It's a little white box looking
thing with a picture of a bottle of...Malibu, I
think it is. I gathered a few twigs earlier and
set them down on the concrete in front of me. It

219

Darkness

takes a few attempt to get them to light but
once they do, I feel bathed in light. Maybe it
was a stupid move to light a fire out in the
open but there are more important things.

I am freezing and there are no houses for miles
around. To either side of me, there are miles
and miles of fields. Cows. I can see hundreds of
cows. I haven't seen many of them; only when we
went out hunting for beef or lamb which was
every month on the middle Saturday. There was
little need to hunt for meat anymore than that;
we mainly ate tinned stuff so fresh meat was a
welcome relief for a few days.

I am hungry but if I wanted to, I could kill one
of them and spit roast the meat but no. I have
survived with out food for longer and the
Prontosil has robbed me of any appetite I may
have had. I just need some water. I feel thirst,
a burning thirst in the back of my throat but no
hunger. I check in my backpack. I have half a
bottle of water; thanks be to...the water gods
or something. I cannot get the cap off fast
enough. The moment I feel the water trickling
down the back of my parched throat, I feel
revitalised. I should conserve my water but I am
likely to come across a river or something. Some
form of running water, at least. I have at least
an eighth left; there is no point in leaving
such a minuscule amount left so I down the rest

of it. I feel better but I am still desperately thirsty but it's a manageable thirst to some extent.

I place the bottle back in the side mesh pocket of my rucksack. I move the rucksack around so when I lie back, it props my head up. A pillow. A lumpy, uncomfortable pillow. I lie back and stares at the sky. The stars. I've always loved the stars. The eternal constants. The sentinels, unmoved by circumstance or chance.

I wish everything was like that.

Darkness

Chapter 22

I wake up to a slight fall of rain. I feel like
I am soaked and the leather in my jacket feels
to be dragging me down. My god, I feel weak. I
think I've pushed myself too far. Emotionally
and physically. I did exactly what I intended; I
cut all ties. I have lost everything for my
pursuit of my own personal truth. I have made my
bed now I have to lie in it.

I roll over onto my side. My bullet wound still
stings whenever I lie on my side but pain is
good. Pain means that I am alive. I pull my
shirt up and examine my wound. I can see the
reminisce of the stitches; on the upside, the

red lines that seemed to stretching out from it, like the branches of a septic tree, have vanished. I examine my wound further. I am lucky to be alive. That bullet should have been my murderer but I conquered. Does that mean that I have, indirectly admittedly, conquered death? I thought that to conquer death is to die but are there other ways?

I've always thought I was special, that there was something...different about me. All of the opportunities I've had to die and I never have. There is a fighter instinct with in me that doesn't want to let go.

There's something else. Something that has been perplexing me. I practically dived at my victim, my infected victim, and I didn't pick it up. One of the reasons the virus allowed a epidemic to unfurl was its hyper-infectivity. You just had to be within several meters of an infected and you were marked for death. I was practically on top of him and I got out of it with just a bullet wound.
I should be infected.

You understand what I mean about something different about me. But there is an alternative. An alternative I had not considered. Maybe he wasn't infected. I mean the symptoms can prevail in other diseases like tuberculosis or lung

Darkness

cancer. Did I kill an innocent man? Did I just
kill in self defence? Would I have killed him if
I had known that he wasn't infected?
The answer to all of them is yes. He would have
killed me and wouldn't have thought twice; I
mean he ripped a hole in me and didn't even
shudder. That's what this world does; it makes
monsters out of us all. The young, the old. The
indifferent. No one is safe to the effects of
this world.

I shudder.
It's bloody freezing.
It can't be later than dawn so morning dew
begins to colour the endless fields, being
chased by an omnipresent mist. I need to start
another fire. Either that or I need to get
moving. I have a few hours of darkness still on
my side, I could probably find something.

Then something catches my eye. A horse. Among
the cows. Disguised like a wolf in sheep's
clothing. I'll get further with a horse; it
looks quite small which makes it just the right
height for me. I have no foot stool to get me
onto the animal. But if I want to get on the
horse, I have to brave...the cows. They creep me
the hell out. The way they just stand there,
lowing at you, liquid pouring out of their
backsides. The horror. The horror.

Darkness

There is no fencing between us so it's just a
matter of plucking up the courage to walk
through them. Do cows charge?
So this is nature. Wide open spaces and the
stench of cow shit in the nostrils, what a
wonderful region.

I get onto my feet and sling my backpack over my
shoulder. It takes me a moment to reclaim my
balance. I walk, cautiously, towards the horse;
it seems to be grazing among the cows. As soon
as I get 10 meters away from the cluster of
animals, they all turn. Staring at me with their
demonic little eyes. All of them, just gazing. I
haven't been this unnerved in a while, it's like
having demonic livestock glaring into my soul.
Oh damn. They're going to charge. Damn. I'm
about to be shish kebabed by livestock. What a
way to go, huh?

But they just remain, staring at me.
I continue to walk towards the horse, who seems
to be breaking away from the crowd. I can cut
around them. I finally reach the horse but it
seems almost tame. He bows his head to me, yes
he is most definitely a boy, and I stoke his
head. Aw, he's not too bad. Most feral animals
would have bit my hand off but he seems
affectionate, almost. I put my hands on his back
and push myself up onto his back. Oh yes, I've
still got it.

Darkness

I have to set off now. I just kick his side
gently and we're off. Yet again, the wind
rushing through my hair, nice sensation. He's
such a nice horse. Aw look at that, I gone made
a new friend. The speed at which I am travelling
is immense. This is freedom. I should be able to
travel a few miles before midday and then I can
stop and get something to drink. My appetite is
returning which is not a good thing. When I get
hungry, I get irritable and my judgement becomes
clouded.

Civilisation. Or a lack there of but it's still
a small town. Or used to be from what I can
tell. Quite a few of the houses are nothing more
than smouldering ash. Recent. So until recently,
people were living here. Fire is a sign of life.
Unless you consider wild fires but the
conditions are never right for that kind of
thing in England. Not warm or dry enough. People
tend to burn their accommodation when they leave
to cover their tracks, which makes no sense.

Unless you consider the last outbreak at the
camp. A boy got infected and it spread like
wildfire. We had to burn the place down; a way
to potentially kill the virus before it could
claim anymore people. As I said, so many times I
could have been infected and I never have been.

Darkness

I felt sorry for the kid. He was sweet; never
hurt anybody, thought he could survive his
entire life without raising his hand to anyone.
I mean, he was a little git but he was a
pacifistic little git and I have to respect
that. Well, I don't because he's dead but I want
to. We used to be a group of over 30, separated
between two buildings. Fifteen people died in
the space of three days. Not all because of the
disease.

You have to understand. Everyone is that
building was a threat. Every single one of them
was marked for death and I know it seems extreme
but they had to be 'disposed' of. Rita was the
one to do it. To light the flame. No wonder she
is messed up. I should give her more credit and
I would if she wasn't, you know, a complete
bitch.

I can still hear them scream.
Piercing. The sound of agony was clear as a
bell. There were older members of the group and
kids. The oldest to die was 23 and the youngest
was 8. It had to be done but sometimes the right
thing is the hardest thing to do. Doing the
right thing should not be easy otherwise it
isn't right. The right thing should not benefit
you but torture you. Consume you with false
justification. An old friend taught me that and
if I could remember them, I would be in a better

place.
I like the smell of smoke. You'd think that
after having my nostrils filled the smell of
burning fat and flesh would turn my stomach
against it but it doesn't. There's
something...warm about the smell. Well obviously
but there is something comforting about it. I
have convinced myself that someone close to me
must have smelt of smoke but what do I know?

I walk up to a building, unaffected by the
flames, that appeared to be an old theatre. At
least, that's what I can make out from the
decrepit neon lights that remained. This place
would have been a sight in the old days; with
the neon lights, this sign would illuminate the
dark. There was a little community theatre by
our base and I would go there sometimes; to get
away from everything and to focus on things.
There was this chandelier, made of crystal, and
it must have been there for decades. It looked
so out of place with the antique surroundings
and the roof that looked like it was caving in.
Moss and damp seemed to own the walls and every
visible surface but this bloody massive
chandelier still looked like it had just been
manufactured. A breath of life in a world of
death. That was quite poetic. Go me.

I push against the doors. Jammed.
I place all of my weight against the door,

trying to focus all of the pressure to my
shoulder and into my core muscles. I will get
this bloody door open. Shelter in some respect.
My plan of pushing against the door is failing
miserably so I try another approach. I stand
back. I run at the door and...it falls in. I
land right on my stomach. Ow. My chest. Ow.

I have to admit, I've had better ideas under the
circumstances but oh well. You only live once,
am I right? Not that you would know because if
you knew, you would be dead so would have the
capacity to agree with me or not. That would be
unfortunate for all parties involve because you
would be deceased and I would be a psychic which
would suck.

Anyway I compose myself and walk forward. This
is going to sting in the morning but it stings
now anyway so I guess I just have to accept this
'turn of events'. Ha. I was asking for it I
suppose. Oh if they could see me now. Reeking
and looking half crazed. I would imagine I am
quite a sight. I am definitely not attractive in
the slightest.

The wood has rotted. The air stinks of damp. Not
unlike everywhere else in this country. It is
amazing how all the building disintegrate within
a matter of years when humans do not maintain.
It's like a larger scale version of the fall of

the Roman Empire. The fall of the human empire, not because of implosion but because of a virus. Humans always pretended like they were at the top of the food chain like the Romans had the most powerful empire in human history. Both wiped out because of the stupidity and the ignorance to believe that they were invincible. Both got what they deserved in the end as is inevitable.

It is a rather fitting analogy when you really think about it. I am quite proud of myself for that...realization. Oh my god. I can see them. Gum balls! It has been years since I have seen them; John retrieved them on a hunt one time. There were like, hundreds of these little multicoloured spheres. Everyone went mental about them, eating their share on that day. I conserved mine for years. I loved just looking at them; not so crazy about the taste. It also seemed so...synthetic. But at this rate, I am so famished I am considering eating graze so take from that what you will.

I should probably try and find something else for Barnabus. My new friend. Who happens to be a stallion who was trying to get a bit overzealous with me. Men. They're animals...quite literally. Even though I'm not overly fond of bestiality if I'm being honest.
This place though. It is breath taking even

though time had eroded most of its beauty but it
still survives to the edge of doom itself. I
could stay here for the night, set off tomorrow
at midday. I have few choices left but where I
stay is one of them; one of the things I can
dictate over.

I walk into A. A is an arrangement of stalls and
a massive stage. Slight problem, it has no roof.
It has no roof. It has no bloody roof. What
happened? Did someone decide to go to the effort
of climbing onto the roof and knocking it down?
Why would you do that? Dick move right there.
Dick move.

This must be one of the areas most affected by
fire damage or human damage. Why would you
disrupt a form of shelter that had some subtle
beauty? I guess people can only think of
themselves, not about the implications of their
actions on the poor sods,like me, who run to
survive. Why would they even care about anyone
else? It's not like we're interdependent
anymore; we tried being reliant on each other
and look what became of that. Blood stained
walls and the pavements corrupted by vomit and
disguised by blood spatters.
Another reason in the encyclopedia of why
everything sucks.

I open one of the fold up chairs in a section of

the stand that still has a roof. I can feel the damp texture of the seat, tearing through my trousers, but I don't move. There are worse sensations and I have not the energy to give a shit about things. I lean back and close my eyes. It's too late to go back; I am too far gone as it were. Two days I've been gone. I wonder how they are. I mean, the kids annoy the crap out of me but I guess I do miss them. I pity them also. I got lucky because I had John find me and take me under his wing as it were. Others were not so lucky.

I wonder how Roman is. I know I shouldn't because of the state of our relationship at the current time but that does not stop me. I do miss him. His melodramatic and, occasionally, snidy remarks. Then again, I don't know if I miss him or human companionship which is saying something because I mindlessly dislike people because I have been screwed too many times.

Anyway, I have to focus on the issue at hand. The past is in the past. Roman and the group are in my past but this is my future. My chance to rediscover myself without being told who I am by someone who was enamoured with me.

I wake with a start. The door creaks open. It could be a feral animal but it does not sound like it. They sound like human footsteps. I can

Darkness

hear the sound of weapon hitting someone's hip
as they walk.

Damn it. Please don't come down here. I duck
down. I should have thought of something else
but I am panicking. They are getting too close.
I can't leg it out of here.

"Lexi? Is that you?"

Yes, it's me but who the hell are you?

Chapter 23

"Lexi? Marcus, get your arse down here now; I think we've found her."

How the hell are these people? I don't recognise any of the voices so it's not anyone from the camp. I don't fraternise with any other groups and we've always been careful to never use full names when on a hunt. Who are they and why are they looking for me? This makes no sense. Do I fight, run or allow myself to be subdued? I want to know why they were looking for me; do I really want to burn my bridges before they've been formed?

I stand up slowly, surveying my surroundings and escape routes. Suddenly, I'm surrounded. Claustrophobic, surrounded by people, not good. Extremely very not good. They just stare at me. Why are they staring at me? That unnerves me

more than if they just tried to attack me. At
least my thoughts would be justified in some
regard, would they not?

I stare directly at the one who was shouting to
me. I definitely have no idea who she is; she
looks relatively young. She has facial features
that can only be described as rodent like. She
has her ginger hair scraped back off of her face
which doesn't help mask her distinguished nose.
She appears to have been talking to a walkie
talkie. Who are you?

"I knew we'd find you. Come on dear, we have
someone you need to meet..."
She extends her hand to me but I back further
into the corner. I am not going anywhere with
them; if they want me to meet someone, they can
come to me.
"Come on, there's nothing to be frightened of
Lexi. My name is Linda and this is my group. We
want to help you Lexi..."
"My name is Elektra. I am not going anywhere
with you. Someone wants to meet me, tell them to
come to me themselves. I am not going anywhere
with you."

"Come on...Elektra. If you'd prefer for us to
call you that. We can get them to come down here
if that would make you more comfortable. You
have no idea how long we have been searching for

you."

No. I don't have any idea because I have no idea
who the hell they are. I recognise none of these
people. I do not understand why they have been
searching for me and I do not want to get
involved. This frightens me. Unnerves me. But I
can't let it show. I won't give them the
satisfaction of seeing me frightened.

"Yes, I would prefer to be called by my name.
No, I don't have any idea. Bring them to me. Go
on. Go on and talk to people."

She smiles. She's smiling at me. Why the hell is
she smiling at me? Did I say something funny?
When I use my obnoxious tone of voice that is
usually the clearest indication I can give that
it is not wise to ridicule me. Why is she not
taking the hint? That smile is even more
unnerving and the other bastards are still
staring at me. Pointing their guns. Bastards.
This is still scaring me.

"Of course, I'll get him. He needs the exercise
anyway. You have the spark, I can tell. Ha. It's
no trouble; Jason, look after her and try not to
lose her."

This gangly creature with hair like a mop walks
over to me and places his hands around my arm.

Darkness

Jason can shove his hand where the sun don't
shine as far as I am concerned. He better let go
off me or he won't have his hands for much
longer. I am not going to struggle. However, I
just stare at his hands, almost burning into
them. It has no effect and I don't know what I
hope to achieve but it's not going to stop me.

He's not too bad looking when he moves his hair
from his eyes. He has these cornflower blue
eyes, I am a sucker for eyes as you may have
gathered, and a strong, squared jaw. He is
handsome in his way. Not in the same way as
Roman is but in a different way. Roman's
attractiveness comes from the way he knows he is
handsome and his personality. Jason seems to
have an element of coyness which is attractive
in itself. I sound like such a slut sometimes
but then again, I haven't had a great of choice
before.

"So...how's it going?" That must be the worst
attempt at a start of a conversation that has
ever been established. Why am I talking to him?
I mean, I don't know him and the way he is
gripping at my arm is making the atmosphere so
awkward.
"I am well, madam. You?"
He's polite, I'll give him that much. Ugh,
madam? Really? I have never been referred to as
madam and I'm not sure I want to be referred to

it now. However, he has a gun and, since my last
run in with a man with a gun, I may as well be
amiable.
"Good good...well the weather's been a bit
unreliable which has been inconvenient but apart
from that..."

The door opens again. I look over and see an
aged man with wavy grey hair. He walks aided by
Linda and his eyes do not leave me. He seems to
be almost analysing me. Well at least I know I
am not in any danger; what harm can he cause me?
Stare me to death? Well there did used to be the
expression 'if looks could kill'.
I still have no clue who he is. How does he know
me? This perplexes me.

After five minutes, he finally reaches me. I
still have no idea who he is. He appears well
groomed under the circumstances. No stubble. His
hair is not too long considering. His grey eyes
pierce my soul. There is something almost
crystalline about them. Something dead or
precious, I'm still trying to decide.

He just stares. If only he knew how much I hate
people staring at me. How uncomfortable it makes
me. Then he places his hand against my cheek. I
know him. There is something in the back of my
mind that is screaming that I know him. Why can
I not remember him? I don't pull away from him

but now, I'm aware of how I am staring at him.
Reciprocating his analytical gaze.

His eyes seem to be filling up with tears and a
smile creeps on his lips. I feel like I should
be mirroring his emotion but I can't. Why can't
I remember you? I feel guilty for not being able
to muster this emotion. He whispers:
"Elektra?"
I nod. It's all I can do. I mean it is my name
but still, how does he know me? Even if he knows
me from my past, I have changed. Changed
massively over the period of ten years. I would
be unrecognisable from the frightened child
cowering in the shadows.

He draws me into a warm embrace. He hasn't
gotten the hint that I have no clue whatsoever
who he is. I can't force myself to pull away
from him. Something about this feels natural.
There is some form of connection but I cannot
comprehend what it is.

He then pulls away from me and stares yet again.
Why are you not telling me who you are? Are we
playing the ambiguity game? I am not going to
ask him; I'm sure I can figure it out somehow.

"Marcus, we need to clear out. This building
looks unstable. We can sort things out at the
base."

Darkness

Linda's voice breaks this illusion of happiness.
I was almost swept up in the moment but I have
been brought back down to Earth. Who are you,
'Marcus'?
"Yes, of course. We need to clear out; Jason,
look after Elektra will you? I trust you will
make sure she is alright and try to be less
sullen."

Oh yes, my friend Jason. Jason with his
unnaturally long nails and firm grip. Well,
maybe I should go with it. My gut reactions have
served me well thus far, well I say that. They
haven't really but it is the only reassuring
thought in my brain. He takes a hold of my arm
again and we walk. Marcus seems to run off,
aided yet again by Linda. This might not be too
bad, I hope.

My horse. Where did he go? What did they do with
my damn horse? My poor Barnabus. Wait, there are
cars. Actual cars that were not there when I
entered the building. No way do this group have
petrol; that is bloody amazing. I have never
actually been in a car but I will admit, it may
be a welcome change to walking or cycling or
riding horse that want to ride you.

Jason walks around to the side of this Smart car
and opens the door for me. Riding shotgun. Okay
then. The rest of the patrol file into this

people carrier so it looks like it is just going
to be Jason and I. Time to get to know each
other, if that was the intention. It is
admirable that he is such a gentleman, opening
doors. I get into the car and the smell is
intoxicating. It smells like...leather I think.
But the seats are felt. Contrast right there.

When Jason starts the car, after a few
splutters, it actually starts. That excites me
right off of the bat. A working car. This is
amazing! My simple delight must have been
registered on my face because Jason turns to me
and says:
"Never been in a car before, madam? It is better
than other forms of transport but this is a
rarity. It is difficult to produce the quantity
of petrol needed."
"Yeah, my first time. You're telling someone who
has ridden a horse for over 15 miles; there are
definitely better forms of transport. So, how
long have you know Marcus?"
"Really? Ever since my mother died when I was
12. I had no other choice and Marcus was
incredibly kind to take me in. He could have
left me to die but he gave me a chance to live.
I owe that man a lot. Why do you ask?"
"You didn't answer my question. Well, you did
but vaguely. How old are you anyway? You are
extremely well spoken which is rare from what I
have seen. You speak like you are from the

Darkness

nineteenth century."

He expels a slight giggle. Not a laugh, a giggle.
"I am 20 years of age and I believe that being well spoken and articulate is a benefit in this world. An advantage. You mustn't have seen a lot then. 20 miles? Where was your old camp then? I gather you ran from them, would I be right with that assumption?"

"True enough. Yeah, you would be right there. Towards Blackheath, I think. I was never too concerned with destinations, to be honest. That's what John, the man who took me in, taught me. Never concern yourself with where you are, but where you are going. I don't know either so I don't know where that puts me."

I start laughing when I realise how cynical I sound. I forget how I must appear to those who do not know me. He smiles as well. He has a nice smile. Mind on the task in hand, Elektra. Damn it, ha. Can't blame a girl for looking.
"It puts you in the best position out of all of us. You have an adorable laugh, have you every been told that?"
"What do you mean? Jason, I do believe that you are flirting with me."
Red begins to paint his cheeks.
"Am I really so indiscreet?"

Darkness

"Yes."

We continue laughing. It provides a contrast, true enough. It's gone from being awkward to feeling like we are old friends. It feels different for me to be so comfortable with someone I have just met. This is different because I feel I can trust him. Trusting strangers is a very dangerous thing. Why can I trust him so easily?

It is an hour drive until we reach their bunker. We spend that hour just chatting, getting to know each other. Jason is 20 years old, he joined the group after his mother became infected. They thought he was infected as well but he survived. His favourite season is Autumn, just like mine. He believes that the way to survive in this world is to be intelligent and never to underestimate anyone, or to overestimate them for that fact. He has never really fraternised with many girls which is why Marcus told him to look after me. Looking after a pretty girl. Ugh, the words make me cringe. After all of that, he still knows very little about me. What can I say? I am a very vague person.

"Come on, there must have been a time when you thought 'what is it all for?' Do not deny it, you must have thought of it. What are your

thoughts about the purpose of life?"
"Well, I haven't. It's depressing to think about
it. We're born, we live, we die. What more is
there? It's what you do in life that matters.
Alright then, you asked the question. What is
your great philosophical argument for life?"
" I believe that we are here to pay penance for
the actions of our ancestors. Say your
grandmother was a murderer or a petty thief, you
would have a tougher time of it in this life."
"But everyone has had a crap time of it in this
world."
"My point exactly. Humans are awful."
"True that. You may have a point there."
" You are more intelligent than you give
yourself credit for, you know that Elektra. I
sense you have a self- deprecating air about
you."

"Piss off. I thought Marcus put you with me
because you were awkward around the female sex;
you seem to be flirting with me like nobody's
business."
He begins to blush again. I think I may have
insulted him.
"Why wouldn't I flirt with you? You are
incredibly beautiful. I have no idea where it
comes from. I am sorry if I seem to be too
forward but I have to speak my mind."

Now I'm the one blushing. Oh my god, I am

Darkness

embarrassed and I am showing him. I do not know
if I am flattered and embarrassed or if I am
embarrassed and insulted. I love Roman and I
have only just left him. He may be still waiting
for me and here I am, flirting with this gangly,
blonde creature who seems to have taken a shine
to me. I have taken a shine to him, faster than
I ever did with Roman. There is one thing I do
know; Roman hates me now and Jason is a nice guy
but I am here for one purpose, to find out what
these people seem to know about me.

"I am not."
"You are too modest. I am too honest which is my
bane but modesty...that is a danger in its own
right. Underestimating yourself."
"Being honest is advantage; I am a compulsive
liar so I guess we are polar opposites. Let's
agree to disagree."
"Agree to disagree. I will warn you; I am
persistent."
"And I'm stubborn."
"Aren't we an absurd pair?"

When we arrive at the bunker, I realise why they
must have done so well. Their bunker is
underground.
"This used to be a disease research facility.
Like the Centre for Disease Control in Atlanta
but more efficient. We began to preserve the
fuel from the generator and use it for the cars.

Darkness

We have air conditioning and warm water, we have
it good."
"I wish I could believe that but your face is
telling another story, Jason."
"It's complicated."
"It always is."

Air conditioning sounds good but warm
water...that statement wins me over immediately.
The only hot water I've ever had was when we had
baths made from boiling water from the battery
operated kettle. They had me from warm water.

Okay. I am prepared. Let's do this.

We walk through the front doors and...ugh, it's
hot. Where is this air conditioning Jason was
going on about. Ugh...bloody hell, it's humid.
We walk in sync with each other. Left, right,
left, right. There are also a great deal of
lights, probably powered by the generators. It's
nice to be able to see where I am going without
having to rely on natural light.

"Are you ready to see Marcus?"
"As ready as I'll ever be."
He continues to keep his hand around my arm but
now, he's gripping me less. He's being more
gentle because I think he's more confident that
I won't leg it. The walls have been whitewashed
so the walls are so bright, they are painful to

Darkness

look at without feeling like you are about to
lose your vision. Light seems to ricochet from
surface to surface.

Marcus' office is relatively small. It reminds
me of a headmaster's office. The stereotypical
three bookcases and mounds and mounds of paper
files. Rustic, I like. He is sitting in this egg
shaped leather chair and just stares at me. Are
we really playing this game again? Who is he and
why, when he looks at me, does it seem like he
is yearning for me? It makes me feel like even
more of bitch that I can't force myself to
remember his face, even though it feels like it
should carry some significance.

He clears his throat.
"It's been a while hasn't it, my love. It's been
too long."
"Yes, it has been. I am sorry but who the hell
are you? I am done with this cryptic bullshit.
Who are you?"

I was probably too blunt about that. Well, there
is no probably about it. I guess I just have to
speak my mind.

"Oh you probably wouldn't remember, would you?
It's alright, my pet. It's not your fault.
Elektra, I'm your dad."

Darkness

What...the...fuck?

Chapter 24

He's my dad?
My dad?
What the hell?
How? How can I have found him without meaning
to? Why am I so pissed off at myself and at him?
Why am I annoyed at the fact that I can't
remember my own dad?
Oh my god! Can I believe what he's saying? Why
didn't he find me earlier? I have so many
questions which I am owed answers to. That he
can answer now. I am half way between crying and
wanting to break something, so I compromise. I
kick my leg. If I focus on the pain, I won't
cry. At least, I think that's what the method
is, isn't it?

Darkness

"Elektra? Are you still with us?"
"Yes. How? How are you here? You were dead and
then John told me you were alive and then...
how?"
"John. I knew it. I will kill the bastard when I
get my hands on him. He stole you from us. You
were frightened, didn't know how to cope on the
outside and then he took you. You don't know how
many years we have searched for you. From the
moment you left, we never stopped looking. I
couldn't believe you were gone; you have to
listen to me, darling."
"No, I don't. I don't have to believe you. I
don't have to believe a word that comes out of
your mouth because I don't know you. I have no
recollection of you!"
"I understand. This must be a shock but there is
no need to overreact."
"Overreact. This is not overreacting! This is me
being calm and rational! Do not tell me you
understand because you don't have a fucking
clue! I have believed I was an orphan for ten
years! You have no idea and I will overreact if
I please!"

I am so melodramatic but can you tell me that I
am wrong? Don't I have that right? My anger is
not directed to the right person but it pisses
me off that people think they understand what I
am going through. Who can honestly say that they
have thought themselves an orphan for ten years

Darkness

then to find their father and not to recognise them? Not many.
I am angry with John which makes me annoyed at myself. John raised me for over half of my life; he taught me everything I know and, most importantly, he kept me alive. He must have had a reason. For taking me away. He must have thought it in my best interest. I can't think of John so badly but I have to, to truly hear what this man who claims to be my father says.

"If you need more time before we can talk, you can go to room 118. Linda will take you. You know where I am when you are ready."
"Thank you." I whisper.

I walk out of this office. He thinks I hate him. I must seem like the biggest bitch imaginable to come out with that to a man who probably thought his daughter was dead or worse. How could I do that to anyone, never mind the father I always wanted to know? But this raises a question, where is my mother?
Were they not together when I was born?
Did she succumb to illness while I was gone?

I am a terrible, terrible person.
Linda walks with me in silence, which I am thankful for. I can feel her eyes burning into the back of my head. It appears that she and Marcus are close in some capacity so it's

natural she may jump to his defence. After walking for what seemed like hours but was, in reality, about five minutes, we arrive at room 118. Linda takes out a key and unlocks the door.

"This room is an en suite. Hot water from 7pm to 11pm. Lights out at 11:30pm. Breakfast is at 8am but it is not mandatory. See you in the morning Elektra."
"Wait. Could you tell Marcus that I didn't mean what I said?"
"You can tell him yourself. Tomorrow. Goodnight. Marcus is a good man who has always done what he could for this group. He would move Heaven and Earth for you and he nearly did. He deserves more respect from a little bitch like you. Good night."

Well, don't hold back Linda. She storms off. I guess I deserve the lecture but she didn't have to be so coarse about it. Damn.

I walk into the room. It's not too bad. Whitewashed with a sense of asepticness. Seriously, it looks like it is so clean that bacteria has no colonies here. It's too clean. Too clean. There is a bed with a metal frame and posts. There is a metal table and, you guessed it, a metal chair. There is nothing about this room that feels warm. It feels to...antiseptic and hostile. Harsh.

Darkness

I walk straight to the bathroom. I need to wash, to finally feel clean after having weeks worth of grime staining my flesh. Everything seems to be made of metal and corrugated iron, including the shower. The shower curtain appears to be a sheet of silver foil but it is too strong and not as ductile.

I undress. Ugh...I feel unsanitary and disgusting. I must have caught myself at some point because my knees have been cut to shreds. I enter the shower and twist every one of the knobs in the hope that water will flow and remove the scum from me. It starts as drips and then develops into a steady flow. It feels breath taking. The warmth hits my skin like a tonne of bricks and seems to liberate me.

I stand there for a minute, allowing the temperate conditions to consume me and seduce me. I watch as the aqueous dirt run down the drain. I take the loofah that sits on one of the shelves in the shower and apply soap to it. It smells like lavender mixed with synthetic lemon. It smells delectable.

After thoroughly cleaning my body, I take this bottle of milky white liquid with a plastic label, saying 'shampoo', and pour it onto my hair. It lathers immediately, conditioning and

Darkness

removing four months' worth of grease and
atmospheric grime.

After five minutes, I get out of the shower and
towel dry myself. For the first time in a long
time, I feel clean and I don't feel consumed and
suffocated by a constant layer of pollution. I
wipe the condensation off of the mirror and look
at myself for the first time in a while. Without
of the grime, I look younger. Clean. Innocent
almost. I've always looked young for my age
which is why I have always felt that I had to
defend myself. Like a chihuahua trying to be
aggressive to prove themselves. A yappy puppy.

I put on my bra and a pair of knickers I found
in one of the drawers. I always thought I was
quite muscular but I have lost a great deal of
weight; illness has robbed me of most of my
curves. I still have relatively big hips and my
breast size seems to be the same. My six pack
has all but vanished and I can see my ribs
poking through my flesh, like a skeletal
glockenspiel. The only thing I have eaten in the
past three days has been a gum-ball so it is
only natural that I would lose a few pounds but
this is drastic. Over analysing myself. Not the
best thing I must admit. Not the best for the
self esteem.

My nose is slightly off centre but my black eyes

are fading and are no longer swollen. I look brutal; I don't see what people see in me. The bruising that paints around my eyes only makes the green more vibrant. I guess I inherited the crystalline nature of my father's eyes. I have his mouth as well. I do resemble him in some ways. Logically, I must have inherited his hair colour as he has streaks of my shade in his hair. With my hair wet, it appears so much longer than before. I don't look so ratty or bemused; I actually look like a normal human being for the first time in forever.

Then again, I don't know that. I know nothing about my past and now, I have met the first person who may be able to answer my questions about what I was like before. I believe him when he says he's my father. I guess I want to believe him because I want to feel like there is someone out there that may know me better than I know myself. Someone who knew me as a child. I made him think that I hate him or maybe he understands why I may be pissed. I'm hoping it's the latter. I will speak to him in the morning and, I don't know, clarify things.
He holds the key to my past.

I lay a towel down onto the pillow and sit on the bed. I run a comb through my hair that I have found in a drawer. I have to tug at my hair a few times to get it through but my hair feels

softer and more manageable. I feel so dead. The
warmth of the shower has lulled me into
tiredness. A full sense of security. I will
allow myself a few hours of sleep and then, I
re-evaluate things.

I lay my head back and stare at the ceiling. The
lack of colour and texture makes it the perfect
canvas on which to project my thoughts.
Everything that is going on inside my mind. I
found him. I had little faith that I would ever
find other colonies of survivors, but the one I
do is the one I have always been trying to find.
Where I have always belonged.

But how have they achieved all of this? How?
This feels like a piece of civilisation in a
broken world. Thinking about how they could have
established this compound causes a profound ache
to form in the centre of my head. I slide off of
the bed and enter the bathroom. I open the
medicine cabinet and examine the items within.
There is a 330ml bottle of TCP, bandages, fabric
plasters and a packet of paracetamol. I look at
the box. Its expiration date hasn't passed yet
so it should be safe. I run the tap to fill a
glass of water and take two tablets. I have
always had issues swallowing tablets, hence why
I prefer paste medicinal relief. Or injections.

I go back to the bed and lie down. I feel drowsy

Darkness

but for the first time, I am not fighting for
consciousness. Sleeping with one eye open.
Fighting for survival.
I am so exhausted.
I allow the darkness of sleep consume me.

I wake to the sound of a knock at the door. I
don't feel dead but I don't appreciate the wake-
up call. The warm silk of sleep has been ripped
away from me and now...I have to face reality
once again. I roll my way out of the bed and
groggily make my way to the door. I scrabble to
open the door.
"Yes?"
"I hate to disturb you but I thought you may
want to know breakfast is being served and
Marcus wants to see you in his office at 11am,"
Jason says, keeping his eyes pointed at the
floor. I must be embarrassing him, I mean I am
half naked.
"Oh, yeah. Thank you," I say as I reach down to
put a white vest that lay on the top of this
laundry basket. I can't find trousers at the
moment but that should make it less embarrassing
on both our behalf's. I guess I am so used to
people having such a casual attitude towards
nudity that I forget that others are not used to
it.

"I could bring you something, if you don't want
to socialise. I have time before my 'patrol'

begins," he smiles at me and begins to wring his
hands "so what do you say?"

"Yeah, if you wouldn't mind. Thanks Jason."
"Elektra?"
"Yeah?"
"Don't feel you have to get dressed on my
account," he winks at me and then walks down the
corridor. He is a little devil, I swear. Why is
he so nice? I mean, since the moment I first met
him, he has been nothing but nice and
gentlemanly. Anyone would think he was trying to
impress me or win me over. Probably because he
is.

I find a pair of tracksuit bottoms and put them
on. They are a little bit big but they will do
for the moment. It's now that I realise how
sweaty I am. The humidity continues to cling to
me. The black tracksuit bottoms attract heat but
I am hoping it will be balanced out by the white
vest, reflecting the heat.

I decide to make my bed. It will give me
something to do for the moment. I have reached
the point of hunger where I can feel bile rising
up through my throat like an alkaline serpent.
Maybe food will vanquish the feeling of my
nausea. I just need to maintain my general focus
on not emptying the minimal contents of my
stomach.

Darkness

I pick up the half full glass of water, that I used to take the paracetamol last night, and walk to the sink once again. I pour the stale water into the sink and watch it swirl down the plughole. I fill up the glass and take a slip. That tips me over the edge and the bile makes an appearance. Luckily, I made it to the toilet in time. The vile alkaline solution almost flies into the water in the toilet. My stomach muscles contract and relax, forcing more of the liquid out of my mouth. It's okay. I usually feel much better once I have vomited, when it comes to extreme hunger.

I take another sip of water and sit down onto the toilet to try and regain my balance; my co-ordination is seriously lacking. I need to breathe. Inhale. Exhale. Inhale...exhale. I am brought back into focus by a knock at the door. I look in the mirror to make sure I don't have any dribble hanging from my chin or draped on the corner of my mouth. I'm good.
"Yes?"
"Room service."
It is Jason. I open the door and am greeted to the sight of two pieces of toast on a plastic plate and, what appears to be, a cup of coffee or tea. It doesn't turn my stomach which is a good sign.

Darkness

"I didn't know what you'd like so I got the general kind of stuff. You do like black coffee, right? We haven't had milk for years on reflection," he says, trying to analyse my reaction and to seek my approval.

"Yes, thank you. You didn't have to get me food; I really appreciate it," I flash a smile and take the plate and coffee from him. Jason stands there for a few moments, smiling at me, before I realise what he wants.

"Please come in. Come on, you've earned it soldier," I say, ending the sentence with a wink. I don't know why I feel so comfortable with him. More comfortable than I every truly felt with Roman or any other man I've been around. I feel like we are old friends who have known each other for years.

"Thank you, ma'am!" He salutes me and follows me into the room. I place the plate and mug on the steel end table and turn around to see him looking at me.

"Have you eaten? My stomach's been a little unsettled so I don't know if I can get through all of this," I declare, placing my right hand on my stomach and walking over to the bed. I continue to look at him and he gazes at me.

"I couldn't unless you insist. Are you feeling ill or...?"

"No, it's just been a while since I had anything in my system that wasn't water. It's my body's

way of telling me to eat, don't worry about me
and I insist."

I take the plate and place it on my lap. I offer
him one of the pieces that had a great deal of
excess butter on it, which is turning my stomach
to look at, and he takes it. He smiles as he
rips a chunk out of the fragment of fried bread.
A dribble of butter slides down his chin. I
reach out to wipe it; he is clean shaven which
is strange. His skin is smooth like silk. No
traces of acne scars or any scars in general. I
can feel heat radiating from his skin.

There is a moment of silence. I keep my hand
there for a moment. The moment begins to become
awkward. I draw my hand away after a few
seconds. Jason then wipes his chin for himself,
while stifling a laugh. He's laughing at me.
He's actually laughing at me. Last time I show
any form of tenderness. This I beseech to
myself.

I, then, decide to take a bite of the lukewarm
toast which settles my abdomen a tad. I take the
time to savour the tastes; the sweetness of the
butter and the grainy elements of the bread. I
continue to nibble at the bread; it's an
annoying habit I have developed, I don't bite, I
nibble. A scarcity of food will do that to you I
guess.

Darkness

After a few minutes of silence, Jason finally speaks:
"Do you feel better?"
"Yes, thanks. I should be fine. Do you know when I can see Marcus? I have some questions that I want answered and I know he can answer them," I try to assert myself but my voice deceives me.
"After you've finished, I can take you to him. He doesn't really sleep and I get the sense that he wants to speak to you as well."
"Thanks."
I take a sip of the coffee. It tastes like aqueous ground dirt. Cold aqueous dirt. I chug the stale liquid, hoping it won't come straight back up. There is still half of it left but the caffeine is starting to ignite my synapses.

I stand up and put on my boots. I turn around and look at Jason.
"Now?"
"Alright. Your wish is my command madam."
"Please, call me Elektra or Lexi. I am not superior to you in anyway; it's probably the other way around to be honest."
"Your wish is my command, Lexi," he grins and offers his hand to me. I accept and link my fingers between his. We begin to walk. I stop to lock the door and then we continue on. There are many people walking around the corridors, wearing overly white, almost military-esque,

uniforms. There is something...peculiar about
this place.

We continue to walk until we reach the door I
recognise. Marcus' office. I can hear the murmur
of voices; I never usually get so anxious but
this is different. This man is my father, if I
choose to believe him. A man who I have yearned
for ever since I can remember. The man with the
key to unlock the riddles of my past.

I take a deep breath.
"Don't worry. You are his daughter, remember
that. He loves you otherwise he wouldn't have
spent the last ten years searching for you. Have
faith in that. If there is something that Marcus
holds above everything, it's family."
"Thanks for the reassurance, Jason."
"Feel free to call me Jace. If I can call you
Lexi, I may return the favour," he says with a
smile. He is genuinely trying to win me over but
it is futile. I do not need male intervention in
my life at the current time. When I was asleep,
I had time to think about my situation. I don't
need a man. I genuinely don't. There is one
thing that I do need and that is friends. I
guess what I really want is a friend to confide
in, not some half-arsed romance that could never
be any more than that. What I felt for Roman was
not romantic love but something more than that.
Something purer that cannot be articulated by

Darkness

the likes of me.

I push open the door to see Marcus sitting in the egg chair. There are no other people in here so I am guessing...he talks to himself? Or there was someone in here who has perfected the art of teleportation and has got the hell out of dodge. "Elektra, this is a pleasant surprise. Please take a seat, we have much to discuss," he says with a forced pleasant tone, from what I can infer.
"That we do," I reply in kind.
"I will leave you two to it," Jason whispers as he leaves the room.

Darkness

Chapter 25

There is an undeniable moment of tension where
the silence poisons the air.
He clears his throat.
"So, did you sleep well? I know it's all a bit
clinical but it serves a purpose. We think of
ourselves as a military base and it has served
her well so far."
"Alright, thanks. Ah, hence the whole 'yes sir,
no sir, three bags full sir' full act. I get it
now even though maybe it would be more
hospitable without everyone having a broom
shoved up their arses. So bloody uptight."

"Yes, I guess they are," he releases a small
breathless laugh and continues, "you are
referring to Jason, would I be right? He is a

nice boy but he needs to learn how to remove the
aforementioned stick from his backside. I did
not teach him that, just in case you want to
blame me for that."
"I wouldn't dream of it, father dear. Now, let's
cut the crap; I have questions, you have
answers. Let's put them together to create
clarity."
That was rather more poetic than I was
expecting. Go Elektra.

" Ask away. You think you're the only one with
questions? I want to know what my daughter has
been through the past ten years. You ask a
question, then I do. Total honesty. Ladies
first."
I have so many questions. Of all the questions I
want answers to which do I want to ask first. Of
course I know. The question that has been
tearing at the inside of my mind ever since I
can remember.

"What was I like as a child?"
"You were the sweetest little thing. You were
always so wide eyed and curious. Image of your
mother, you were. You still are, so like her. I
never thought you'd grow up but looking at you
now, the strong young woman you've become. I'm
proud of you, so proud."
I look like her. The words I always wanted to
hear from my father. He is proud of me but then

again, he doesn't know me. He knows nothing
about me. That raises another question that has
been nagging at me. It's only half complete.
"What happened to her?"
"No, one question. It's my turn now. What was
your old group like?"

What do I tell him? Do I tell him about Rita?
Roman? The kids? It is still a sensitive area
that I don't want to delve into. Does he really
want to know or is this just small talk?

"Yeah, they kept me alive which I am grateful
for. Anything I am comes from them. Roman, the
eldest member of the group, was...more than a
friend but I had to leave them. I am an adult
and I needed an escape. I wanted to find you.
And my mother. You spoke about her in past
tense, what happened to her?"

I feel that was sufficiently vague.

"She became ill a few months after you were
taken-"
"Infected?" I interrupt
"No, a different kind of ill. Mentally ill. Felt
like it was her fault. I was the one to find
her. Hanging. From a tree a few metres outside
of the compound. She didn't snap her neck so she
would have suffocated. You have to understand,
you were our little girl. The only thing that

mattered to us was keeping you safe and ignorant. We wanted you to be a child for just a little while longer. It was John who convinced us to take you out there."

"John? John never mentioned he had ever been part of another group. He said the group he had founded was the only one he had been in."

"Then he's a fucking liar like he always has been!"

Sensitive area. I think that has successfully been established. How could John have been involved in my parents' group? More importantly, if he knew my parents and they seemed to value his opinion, why did he take me from my parents? Why did he want me to know about the ins and outs of this world before I should have? Was that even his plan? The man with the real answers if nothing more than ash.

"Excuse my language but everytime I think about what that man did, what he caused...if I every find him, I will kill him."

"No need. He topped himself a few weeks ago. That's how I found out that you might be alive; he let that slip before he took his final breath. So there's one less job. I am sorry; no one should have to see someone they love take their own life."

I want to sound bitter. Resentful towards John which is what my father wants to hear. That I hated John and, in the end, wanted him dead but

Darkness

I can't. Knowing that John lied to me doesn't
change the fact that he raised me and tried to
protect me as a daughter. I can't hate him. It
is not physically possible.
He sighs and rubs his brow. My tone deceived me.
I can't feel the way Marcus wants me to feel
because our experiences in the world are so
different. He saw one side of John and I saw the
other.

"Were you and John close in some capacity?"
"He was my mentor, so yes. We were close which
isn't exactly what you want to here but it is
the truth. I understand he lied to me about
everything in hindsight but he was a good man.
What was John like, when he was a part of your
group?"

I have to know. I don't want to know but I have
to. It may help me to understand why he did what
he did. Why he felt he had to lie to me about
everything. I have to understand.

"John? He was...different. He was infatuated
with you and your mother. He was quiet, that is
all I can really say about him. I always sensed
there was something...unwholesome about his
relationship with you. It made me uncomfortable
because you were just a little girl. I should
have done more to stop him; maybe I could have
avoided all of this..."

269

Darkness

"Don't you dare blame yourself! If it brings you any peace, John probably would have taken me no matter what you did, I think. Now define unwholesome."
I swallow all of the excess saliva that has built up in my mouth. I am starting to feel physically sick but it was my choice. To tarnish a dead man's memory.

"I can't help myself," he says, adjusting his position, "he used to spend a lot of time with you. He would go into your bedroom at night and then he would come out ten minutes later, his flies undone or his shirt untucked...I also suspected there was something else."

"What? Do you mean...he was a kiddy fiddler," I then vomit the contents of my stomach onto the carpet flooring of the room. How could he do that to me? That is a bloody vicious and conniving lie if he is deceiving me. Why would John do that? I refuse to believe it. Wouldn't he have continued once I was a little older? Unless he got off on touching up little children. Oh I feel sick. I feel physically ill.

Marcus runs around the desk, grabs a bin from by the side of the desk and keeps my hair off of my face while I take the bucket. I was a little girl. I was just a little girl. I don't want to believe it but why would he lie to me? What

Darkness

would he hope to achieve but to poison me
against John?

"Bring up Elektra, I'm sorry. I shouldn't have
told you but I thought...I thought maybe you
could take it. He didn't do it to you again
then? When he had you all to himself?"

I try to compose myself while wiping buttery
vomit from my chin. Thought I could 'take' it?
Bullshit. I can't remember anything about my
past and then he springs this idea that a man I
admired used to rape me when I was a child.
Bullshit. I open my mouth but the words won't
come out. I am in shock.

"I...I....," I mutter, trying to articulate my
thoughts. Maybe it's better that I can't
remember my childhood. My innocence was ripped
away from me when I couldn't have even known
what sex was. He violated me. The words repeat
in my head, poisoning each thought in my mind.
Marcus puts his arm around my shoulder. I don't
stop him or pull away; is there the possibility
that he could be lying? I want Marcus to be
lying, making up spiteful stories but there is
something about his tone that makes me think he
is being completely genuine. Ugh, why did I ask?

I guess subconsciously I must have known. My
lucid dream and the hymen incident. Oh my god,

why would John do that to me? Was he using me as a power play over my father? Once he had me, asserting himself over me was made void. If he wasn't dead...I don't know. I just don't know anymore.

"He never touched me, if that's what you're asking. I...I just need a moment. Oh my god, fuck. He never showed any display of physical affection to me; he only hugged me a few times in the ten years I knew him. Fuck," I can just about muster up a mutter. I cannot think of the right words. Is it possible to know what to say? "I'm sorry to bring it up. I have never been able to stop thinking about that bastard, hurting you. I have had the image in my head for the past ten years, torturing me. But, you're alive and he kept you safe and he didn't hurt you. That's one thing," he rubs my back, trying to comfort me but that isn't what I want. I don't want to be comforted; I want to understand why! Why John did it?
I can see where I get it from. Marcus knows how to play people like violins, just like me. He is trying to emotionally manipulate me. I am not buying the bullshit he is trying to sell.

"Yeah," I whisper.
"Your question now," he asks, in a jovial tone.
"How did John steal me? What happened the day I was taken and please...don't....bullshit....me."

Darkness

I cannot take any more lies or deceit. I just want to know what happened; it's in the past so nothing can change it but at least I can understand more about myself and those I've trusted forever.

"It was his idea. To take you with us on a run. John thought you needed to know what it was like out there and your mother agreed. We just wanted you to be a child for as long as possible. You would always play and question things; you were the one innocent thing in our world. Did you ever play once you joined John's group? How long were you a child?" He shifts his weight onto his other foot and sighs. He then decides to sit back down into the chair.

"Anyway, we took you with us. You were frightened but you were still like this ball of flaming energy. We were about 2 miles away from the compound. You, John, your mother and I. We suspected nothing. John called for you and you ran, like a pocket rocket. You idolised him and I never understood why. It was either idolisation or fear, you never made it clear. Next thing we know, he has his hand over your mouth and is pointing a gun at us. You struggled. He let go. The force overpowered you and you fell. You hit your head on the concrete.

He shot your mother in the stomach and he shot

me in the head," he lifts up a bit of hair from his forehead to reveal a jagged scar, "they always said I had a thick skull. I passed out and your mother watched you go, unable to do anything. I don't know what happened after that. I mean what I said Elektra; there has not been a day over the past ten years that I have thought about you and the woman you became. I always knew you were alive. Paternal instinct if you will."

A scar like mine, in a way. Carved by a bullet's path. My kidnap was premeditated; he made my mother watch as he took me while she lay, hopeless. No wonder she lost it because she felt like she failed me. I still feel sick. This is a game changer. Complete bloody game changer. He tried to kill my dad. He probably would think that they were dead and that it was his bullets that severed their life cords. I genuinely wanted John to come out of this smelling of roses but now...I can't feel anything but contempt for that man. I hate him and that is something I never thought I would feel. I hope he rots, the evil, pedophilic bastard.
But I don't.
I don't know what I want to believe right now.

"Matching father daughter scars, ironic," I say with the essence of a smile. I lift up my top, exposing my bullet wound. Dad walks up to me and traces the line of my scar and, then, looks up at me.

"Who did this to you?"

"You think this is bad, you should see the other guy."

Am I really cracking a joke at this moment? But then again, I am stating a fact. I may have an ugly looking scar but at least I'm not worm meat.

He takes me in his arms and forces me into a tight embrace. I reciprocate. I guess this is what I need: comfort. I want my father. I need time. I have to go. I have had the questions I needed answered, answered.

"Please excuse me, I need some air. I will...see you later."

"Okay, see you," he moves to kiss my cheek but I move away before he has the chance. I am repulsed by male contact at the moment.

I walk over to the door and walk out into the corridor. I walk, not focusing on any of the details around me. I am pretty good at remembering routes so I find my room in a relatively speedy time. I open the door to my room and then lock it behind me. Damn. I still cannot believe everything I have heard.

John is the other father figure I can remember having and now...what? Am I supposed to just accept the fact that John was mentally damaged? There have been things he has said, in the past, that were bizarre and should have warranted concern but that was just the way he was. Did I even know John at all?

I don't want to think about it. Any of it. I know the answers that I have been searching for which provides some liberation from my ignorance. I am more unnerved than every but I can no longer claim ignorance. I just can't understand why. Why? Why?

I slop down onto the bed. I need to compose myself and I have no idea how. Everything I thought I knew is a lie. Is there any truth in what I know? I look up at the ceiling. It's becoming more and more difficult to breathe. Small rapid breaths escape from my lungs. I feel like I am hyperventilating. My eyes begin to burn and burning hot tears spill over. Great heaving sobs leave my chest. I can't deal with this. I am not detached; I am too involved with this. Why did I chose to find him? I could have lived in ignorance for the rest of my life. Now I feel dirty. I feel violated by a man who I trusted with my life.

Oh my god.
I am sobbing like an overgrown child but I've earned that right, I feel. I can't control my

Darkness

breathing. How is anyone supposed to know how to
bear that knowledge? I deserve this. I mean I
wanted honesty and I wanted answers. How the
hell can I complain? But did I deserve it? Did I
deserve to be used as some form of power play?
Did I deserve to know this?

I have to get up. Compose myself somehow. I
can't deal with these emotions right now. I walk
over to the wall and proceed to hit my head on
the wall. Again and again. I'd rather feel
physical pain than this psychological agony I
have been forced to endure. I can't deal with
this. I don't want to. I am not ready to deal
with this.

My head is becoming cloudy. I can see blood on
the wall were my head comes into contact with
it. I have to stop but I can't force myself. I
am hoping that this will help me lose
consciousness. I pause. I know what I have to
do. I hit my head again on the wall with such a
force that the world goes black.

Chapter 26

I feel like hell when I wake up. I guess I would considering I have probably killed more than a few brain cells and I can't afford to lose the ones I have. I put my hand up to my head. I feel dried blood on my forehead. I move onto my knees and force myself to my feet. I think I moved too fast. I am so disorientated. I walk into the bathroom and look in the mirror, squinting.

The side of my face is smothered in blood. I have a massive graze on my head that has begun to clot and solidify. I look like hell. I look like I have been in some kind of confrontation. Yes, a confrontation with a wall. Ugh, I feel like hell. But now, I guess, pain is at the forefront of my mind, quite literally.

I hate this. I just want to pretend like no one

of this has happened because ignorance is ultimate bliss from my experience. I just...don't want to talk about it. What I really need is a distraction. Jason. I run the tap and splash my face with the freezing cold water from the pipes. My head stings and my nose burns but I feel refreshed. How long have I been out?

I walk out of the bathroom and speak of the devil, there is a knock at the door. Companionship. I open the door but first, I make sure that my fringe covers the graze on my forehead. I don't need the added aggravation of people questioning me.

It's Jason. What a bloody coincidence.
"I saw you run out of Marcus' office earlier; I was just wondering if you were alright. You looked pretty shaken up. Are you alright?"
He looks genuinely concerned. I am not dragging him into the shit storm that is my life.
"Yeah, I'm fine. I overreacted but I feel like I know Marcus a lot better. You have no reason to be concerned about me Jason; I'm a big girl, I can look after myself," I say as I flash him my falsest smile. He seems to be lapping it up like a puppy. My forced smile seems to invoke a genuine smile in Jason.

He takes my hand and looks me in the eye. Oh

shit.
"I am a lot of things, Lexi, but I am not
stupid. Tell me what happened, please."
Is he pleading with me to get involved in my
life? He can piss right off with that plea. Why
are people unable to grasp the concept that I
don't want them involved with every part of my
life?
I take his other hand.
"I am fine, Jason. Don't worry about me; you
don't have to get involved in this. Why are you
so interested in me and my story?"

He stares at me. He is bloody intense, I'll give
him that. I am not sure where this is going but
the silence is perturbing me. He moves closer to
me, forcing our arms to bend in unison. He bends
his head down until his lips touch mine. His
lips are gentle and he barely places any
pressure on my lips. I pull away. I can't. I
just can't.

"I'm sorry Jason."
I turn my back; I can't bear to look at him. He
is a genuinely nice man who shouldn't be forced
to become involved with the likes of me. He
deserves better than me. In addition to that,
he's only known me two days. He doesn't know
anything about me.

"It's alright. I was being too forward; I

understand if you aren't interested in me but be honest with me, that's all I ask of you. Are you interested in me?"

"No...I mean yes...I don't know okay! I don't know how I feel about you. I have known you two days, Jason. You hardly know me. I am interested in you as a friend; that's what I need right now. Why are you even interested in a girl you know nothing about?"

"Because you are not like any other girls I have ever met. You are the first funny, beautiful girl that I have met while at this compound; why would I not be interested in you? I understand if you just want to be friends," he states with a down trodden expression. He genuinely thought there was something blossoming between us but I still have to consider how I feel and Roman.

"There's another reason as well," I have to be honest with him, it is the least he deserves from me, "in my old group, there was a guy called Roman. He's still out there and I mean...I don't really know where I stand with him. I think I was in love with him. But what I feel is irrelevant at the end of the day, Jason. Don't just hope for the best with me: I am damaged goods and I genuinely believe that you deserve so much better than me."

He appears dejected but he still is not getting the hint. He doesn't understand what I am trying to convey or articulate, I swear. Why does every bloody person I meet think that I am something I'm not? Why do they think that I'm a slut who puts out after two days or that I am strong enough to accept the fact that I was violated as a child? It's sick. All of this is sick.

"You put yourself down too much; I can see that is your issue. I understand; I actually came to fetch you for Linda. Sh e wants you to join us on our next patrol. Are you ready?"
"Alright, let's do this," I mutter. I may as well serve a purpose if I am to stay here. Wait, do I even want to stay here? I mean this is the place where my father is and I have the potential for a love interest in Jason. But the real question is do I belong here This is like a military base and bitch, I did not sign up for that.
But technically, I did just sign up for it so I might as well try my hand at it. If Jason can spend eight years here and turn into the perfect little soldier, maybe this is something I can turn my hand to.

"You may want to wear something a little warmer; it is glacial outside. I will be back in five minutes. Take your time."
He walks away, almost marching. That does make me giggle and I know it shouldn't. I guess

seeing men who are obviously scared shitless of
their own shadow acting as blank canvases.
Acting as if they know no fear. Also, the way he
marches reminds me of...I don't even know what.
He has these long legs that occupy over half of
his body and it looks like something from a
Monty Python sketch. I saw it in a book at this
bookshop I once went on a stakeout to. Ah, I
know what it is: 'The Ministry of Silly Walks'.
They were just images but they raised a smile
out of me. This tall man walking with his legs
far extended and almost galloping. I would give
anything to actually see the sketch but I guess
that is never going to happen. Ah Monty Python.

I walk over to the metal wardrobe that looms in
the corner of the room. There are a few vest
tops, jumpers, jeans, polyester trousers, skirts
and my leather jacket. Someone was in here
because I certainly did not hang it up. My
ironic t-shirt has also gone absent without
leave. Aw bless them, washing my clothes and
sneaking into this room while I'm asleep.
Actually, it is extremely creepy on reflection.

I put on a black jumper over my vest. I am going
to stew. I understand it is bound to be warmer
due to the fact that we are underground but I am
still waiting for this supposed air
conditioning. I take my tracksuit bottoms off

and put on the black polyester trousers in the
wardrobe. I then put on a pair of trainers I
find in the wardrobe as well. Size 3, a
surprisingly perfect fit. I put on my leather
jacket and zip it up. I take a sniff of the
sleeves. I adore the smell of leather and there
are undertones of smoke that remains from
countless cremations.

I may as well make myself look presentable. I
have a hair band in my jacket pocket. I walk to
the bathroom mirror and I tie my hair back into
a high ponytail. I make sure that my fringe
hangs down over the graze and I place it behind
my ear. It still covers it, kind of. I could say
that I had it before; there, I have my excuse. I
can lie about it.

I take another two paracetamol tablets and
swallow them dry. I walk towards the door,
adjusting myself to make sure I don't have any
flesh showing or that my trousers haven't
collected around the top of the trainers. I open
the door and walk out into the corridor. Where
is Jason? It must have been five minutes at
least since I last saw him. I maunder down the
corridor to the left. I will find him at some
point but I have the time, I may as well
explore.

Darkness

There are so many doors. Doorways to who knows
what; well they do but that is beyond the point.
I hear banging. I can't decipher where it is
coming from but it sounds like it is near. Bang,
bang...bang, bang. What the hell? I traipse
forward. The banging becomes a lot clearer: it's
down here somewhere. I have to check this out
now. I catch sight of Roman walking towards my
room; it's now or never. Maybe I can dig up some
dirt on this base? Or...maybe not?

It's in the room next to me. The sign over the
door has been scratched out. I can make out that
it used to say 'storage'. It's either 'storage'
or 'dotigt'; I think storage is the more logical
assumption.

Now, groans from within the stomach of the room
become apparent. They aren't just banging on the
walls; they sound like they are in some form of
pain.

"What are they doing here?" I mutter to myself.
The door is not locked. Why isn't it locked?
From what I can deduce, this doesn't sound like
the kind of thing you want people to stumble
into. I don't like this; something smells fishy
about this. In reality, it actually smells of
meat and almost, bloody.

Darkness

I unlock the door.

There are six people in this room. They seem to just sit in the corner of the room, groaning. What have they done to you?

"Are you alright?" I inquire. In truth, I am utterly terrified. Is this what they do to people who ask too many questions? Ending up in an unmarked room. Light reflects off of the floor and catches my eye. That's blood. There's numerous puddles of blood on the floor. Holy crap. What have they done?

I walk into the room, trying to maintain an air of calm about me. There is no light inside this room which contrasts the whitewashed walls outside. I walk towards the nearest person.

"Are you alright mate?"

I place my hand on their shoulder but there is something...odd about it. They are freezing and the smell is coming from the flesh. It feels...dead.

I don't like this. I don't like this at all. They should be responding, at least acknowledging me. Suddenly this person begins to cough her guts up, quite literally. Solid masses of blood are flung from her mouth. Damn. She

then turns her head to face me but she is
growling. She screams at me which causes me to
jump back. But that isn't what really shocks.
The light from the corridor illuminates her
face. Most of the skins has peeled from her
face. She has no bottom lip as it is hanging
down. Oh my god.

Her eyes have become bloodshot and appear
entirely red in colour. The veins has become
prominent on her skin, painting her like some
kind oil painting. There is something so inhuman
about her. She begins to crawl towards me but
her movement is distorted. She moves like a
spider, arms bent and her arms move faster than
her legs so she is dragging herself along. I
slide backwards, keeping my eyes on her. I feel
my hand land in one of the puddles of blood;
this is nauseating but it helps me along. It's a
good thing I'm wearing black.

She grabs hold of my foot. I kick and kick but
her grips tightens. I keep crawling backwards,
watching her as she seems to be getting faster.
She's trying to bite me. I feel her hyperborean
flesh climb up my leg. She growls and bares her
teeth to me. She has a strip of flesh caught
between her front teeth. What the hell is she
because that is human flesh, I am pretty sure of
it.

Darkness

I don't think I can move fast enough; I have to carry her weight as well as my own. I am so close to the door: I can feel it. I can feel the heat of the lights outside. Just a little further.

I can't move.

She won't let go, no matter how much I kick her. I kick her in the head and a bit of her skull becomes detached but she keeps coming at me. I have never seen this before, in any of the infected. There is the possibility that a mutation may have developed with in the virus. What on Earth are they now? At least the infected used to be people.

Why did I go into this room? Isn't that the mistake that other people have always made? Trusting their instincts to help people and ending up choking on their own blood within a matter of days. She's going to eat me if I don't get away. That's why she's trying to bite me. What the hell is she? A flesh eating zombie? Oh shit. Walking dead? Really?

I turn to face away from her; maybe I can push myself away if I am facing the right direction. Why do I not have any weapons on me? Why did I come in here unprotected? Am I really that stupid...or plain naïve?

I scream. Maybe if I scream, someone will find me before I become food. She is bloody strong. Holding my right leg down and pressing her body weight against me. Maybe this is it.

I close my eyes.

A gunshot rings through the halls.

The pressure on my legs fades.

I open one eye. Jason is standing there with a Winchester rifle, looking content with his kill. I kick the bitch off of my leg. Now she doesn't put up a fight. I stamp on her head to make sure that she is dead because I don't fancy the confrontation round 2.

Jason extends his hand to me.

"I feel like we may have some explaining to do," he says, rubbing his neck with his free hand.

"You think?"

Chapter 27

Once again, I'm in Marcus' office. The walk here was...awkward. Jason had little to say and I was still in shock, trying to figure everything out because I have never seen that before. That...that is not nature. There had better be a bloody good explanation for why someone tried to eat me. I am trying not to see that as a euphemism.

I don't know what to think about it. I mean it is a positive thing because now, I have a distraction but no...no it is not a good thing in any respect. Attack of the cannibals. What the hell?

I feel like I have twisted my ankle. Well I say 'I' but let's face it, it was something to do

Darkness

with the cannibal bitch in the unmarked room. I
understand why it was unmarked now but why it
was unlocked, I don't understand.

"Elektra, you are probably wondering what you
just witnessed," Marcus announces, as if he were
appealing to the masses.
"You could say that...yeah."
Marcus, subject of expertise: stating the
bleeding obvious.
"You don't have to be afraid of them. We have
them under control for the moment. The first
reported case was in January 2028 in Devon. The
first reported sighting of the mutation; we
cannot explain what causes it or why it happens
but it does. One bite or scratch, even a bit of
dribble from their chins, and it's game over.
It's hyper infective and we control it through
our patrols. We are the first and last line of
defence against them, do you understand? If you
want to stay, they are what you will have to
deal with. Any questions?"

Where the hell do I begin? Last defence? They
keep them in a bloody store room. This isn't an
isolated incident either. How many of them are
there? I have to admit, my hopes of there being
thriving colonies of survivors are being dashed.
How come I haven't come across them before? Do
they prefer the sea air or something? None of

291

Darkness

this makes any sense and I don't think there is
any logic to it.

"Alright, how do you kill them? And...when do I
begin?"

I feel like I have just signed my soul over to
the devil so this should be fun.

"You have to destroy the brain entirely. We
think it has something to do with parts in the
centre of the brain and the brain stem. With out
the other parts of the brain, it would cause
them to be animalistic. They die of the
infection that we all know and love and then
they come back. A gun shot is effective but if
you get caught in the middle of them, it draws
them, like a dinner bell. It's better if you use
blunt trauma."

"He means beating them over the head until they
stop moving."

"Thank you for your input Jason," Marcus replies
in response to the interruption. Jason sinks
back like a naughty school child which is an odd
sight, granted, "basically, hit them or impale
them in the head. It's the only way. You start
today. Jason, give her the gun."

Wahey! I get a gun and everything. Jason takes
the Winchester rifle from his belt and hands it
to me. He seems reluctant so I sense that this

gun is of some importance to him. I almost feel
bad about accept it but if it saves my life, I
am going to take it. I'm not insane. I haven't
been tested but I assume I'm not. Anyone who has
claimed otherwise has never been seen again. I'm
kidding...in a way.

"Okay, let's do this," I avow with a smile. It
gets the adrenaline pumping, that's for certain.
I feel like I could belong here and I am too
curious to leave. I have to understand more
about what was going on while I spent my ten
years in a bubble.

Wait, did they know about this? Rita and John?
Is that why we 'had' to cremate everyone? To
prevent them coming back? A bullet to the head
to end them? It's all becoming clear now.
Clarity is a blessing. Thank God I left when I
did. Why have I always been lied to? It really
bloody sucks. I can't tell fact from fiction
anymore.

"Wait. One last question: what do we call them?"

"We call them 'risers'. Original name but to the
point, do you not think?" Marcus says, with an
air of self praise. I assume he came up with the
name. Imaginative.

"No, not really. Might as well call them
'cannibiters' or 'walkers'. Actually, it's to
the point; I guess it's not too bad. Come on,

let's go," I articulate with adrenaline pumping through my veins once again. It feels good to be alive.

"Cannibiters, I like that," Jason interjects, placing his hand around my waist.

"Don't you be getting ideas about my daughter, Jason, or I will remove your meat and two veg alright?"

Jason moves his hand instantly and just links his fingers with mine. Having a father to be protective over me, I can see what I have been missing.

Marcus raises his eyebrow and Jason removes his hand from mine and places it behind his back. I can't help giggling. Things are finally looking up; that is one of the weirdest statements for me to say. I am about to go out and kill 'cannibiters' and I feel invigorated.

That's when things change dramatically.

Next thing I know one of the biters comes up behind Marcus and bites him on the arm, ripping an artery. Blood sprays from the wound and he falls to the floor. I act on impulse and put a bullet in its head. It falls backwards and falls to the floor, with half of its head remaining in the spot where I emptied the bullet. That riser

attacked my dad. It's game over but it can't be.
I only just got him back.

The five other cannibiters that were in the room
have got out. Who left the bloody door open?
Jason is struggling in the corner to rewire this
old tannoy. A riser is getting closer to him; do
I cover him or do I get rid of the others. I
shot the one nearest the door which attracts
them towards me. I have given him some time. For
God sake Jason, hurry the hell up. I have to
keep them away from Marcus as well.

I just keep shooting, hoping that I will hit
something. It's a rifle, it's not meant for such
close range. Shit. I'm out of bullets. There are
still three of them standing and I am not
leaving until all of them are dead.

"Jason,a little help please!"
"I think I've got it," the tannoy begins to work
as I can hear the white noise from here, "we
have a code 3: Amber. Evacuate, everybody
evacuate. We have a man down, man down. Evacuate
now."

The tannoy attracts them to him again. That
gives me more time to select a melee weapon.
That's when I notice the katana above Marcus'
desk. If I can get to that, I may stand a

Darkness

chance. Not that I have ever handled a katana
before.

I pull myself onto his desk and unleash the
beast from its sheath. I have it. It's heavier
than I thought but I can take it. I jump down.
The noise alerts them to me again.

"Come on you ugly bastards!"

Am I genuinely taunting them? Yes, yes I am. The
first one comes at me and I stab it in the eye.
There is something quite satisfying about the
squelch that signalled its end.

I slice the top of the second one's head off
and, once it falls, I kick it to the side. There
is one left. I could let it live; it would be
easy to overpower it but no. This is personal
now. I bring the sword down on the top of its
head, through its face, splitting it's head in
half. I think I've got the hang of this.

"Bloody hell, Elektra. That was astounding.
Wait. Marcus."

I walk over to him. He looks pale and is
convulsing. He looks so different to the
military leader I first met. He looked fragile
before due to his age but now, he looks almost
child-like. I want to protect him, to heal him.
It should be the other way around. I kneel down
and lift his head up. I don't know what I am

supposed to do; this is my dad. This isn't fair. I have only just found him. There is so much I still have to know. We still have so much more of our story left. This isn't fair!

Marcus begins to croak.

"El..lek...tra."

"It's alright dad, I'm here. I'm not going anywhere," I can't help myself from crying, "everything is going to be okay. Just keep your eyes open okay? He's going to be alright isn't he, Jason?"

Jason stares at me uneasily. He doesn't want to say it. He doesn't want to say that it's Marcus' end game. He could at least say something, anything. Give me something, honesty or false hope, I don't care. I just need something to hold onto. I begin to examine the wound and put pressure on it. Pressure will stem the bleed for the moment. I need to buy myself some time until I can stitch it up and disinfect. He's going to be alright, I will not let him die on my watch.

"Jason!"

"I think if you have anything to say, now is the time to say it."

"Okay...okay. I understand. Dad, you can't die on me now. We've only just found each other

again and now, you're abandoning me.
Please...don't die. I can't lose you for real,
please hold on. Please," I begin sobbing as I
articulate the last few words. I can't be an
orphan again. When is it my turn not to be
fucked over by life? When is it my turn? When?
This isn't fair. Then again, life isn't fair. I
should have accepted that by now.

"I...won't leave...you...Elek...," Marcus croaks
and then closes his eyes. No, no, no.

"I love you dad; I'm sorry, please," I whisper
in his ear but I can't feel his breath anymore.
I move my hand, allowing his head to rest on the
floor. I look at my right hand; it is stained
with patriarchal blood. I rub and rub my hand
but it just stains the other. It won't go; it
fades but it still remains like a tattoo.

I look up at Jason. He looks shocked but in no
way emotional. I rise to my feet and look at
him. I feel a steely determination being born
inside of me. This is bloody personal now. The
man with the answers is dead and I don't know
what I am going to do now. An animal is never
more dangerous than when it has been backed into
a corner and that is what *they* have done to me.

"The plan remains the same. You take me with

you," I say, picking up the katana sword, "nothing changes."

"Are you sure that you still want to go? Elektra, your father just died right in front of you. You are in shock; we don't have to go right now. It's alright."

"No, I know what I want. My whole ideology has been shredded to pieces over the past month. I have nearly died twice; lost a mentor and both of my parents; destroyed all my relationships with my past group; discovered these ugly sons of bitches and figured out that I am strong enough to destroy them. I am doing this for me. I am doing this because this disease...this virus has taken everything away from me. If the virus had never come, I could have had a normal life. I could have gone to school; the worst of my worries could have been homework or who I was going out with. I am a monster, Jason. We all are because that is what this world does to us. I understand now.

I also understand something else. I'd like to thank these revolting bastards for the final definitive proof. I have an excuse. The one thing I know as truth. The one thing I see as gospel; this means war."

Darkness

Maybe.
Maybe the choices we make are interdependent. Or
maybe they disappear into a sea of crystal ice
and despair. I've learnt not to regret anything,
however difficult it prevails to be.
I was only young. Young enough that my ignorance
could be excused and glossed over.

I have been lied to my entire life. I can't
trust anyone, I've learnt that. There is only
one truth that has been burnt into my mind;
nothing in this world is clear cut or definitive
and I would like to thank this group for the
final proof.
But I've learnt something else. I can't do this
alone. I can't fight this war on my own but I
can give it a damn good try.

My name is Elektra Daniels; you won't recognise
my world and I wouldn't want you to. This is
only the beginning of my story.

Printed in Great Britain
by Amazon